DRAGON
KNIGHTS

THE
FLAME DRAGON

THE DRAGON KNIGHTS SERIES

THE FLAME DRAGON
THE SHADOW DRAGON
THE STORM DRAGON

DRAGON KNIGHTS

THE
FLAME DRAGON

J. R. CASTLE

Piccadilly
PRESS

For Jamie Samphire,
the deadliest Dragon Knight

First published in the UK in 2015
by Piccadilly Press
Northburgh House, 10 Northburgh Street,
London, EC1V 0AT
www.piccadillypress.co.uk

A catalogue record for this book is available
from the British Library

ISBN: 978–1–84812–459–2
Also available as an ebook

1 3 5 7 9 10 8 6 4 2

Set in Sabon 11.75/17.5pt
Typeset by Palimpsest Book Production Ltd, Falkirk, Stirlingshire

Printed in the UK by Clays Ltd, St Ives Plc

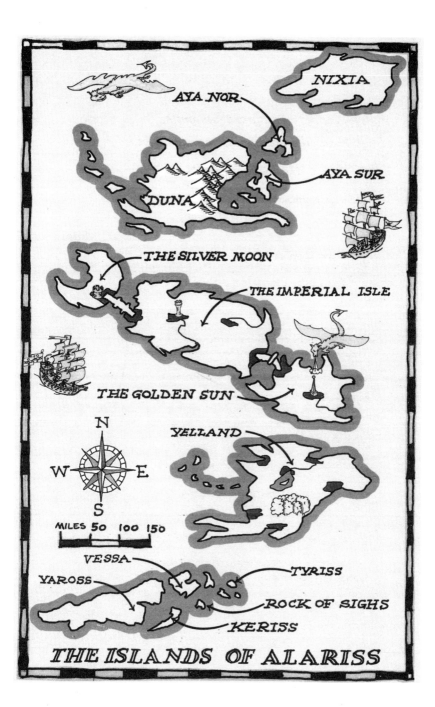

PR⊕L⊕GUE

THE LAST DAYS OF
THE DRAGONS

Vayn stared across the blackened valley. His hard, dark eyes burned with malice, and his scarred face twisted into a vengeful scowl.

The Black Guard had been gathering beneath the Imperial Castle for days, waiting for his orders. Behind the gates and lining the battlements, the last of the loyal Imperial Guard waited for the inevitable attack. The steep stone walls had never been breached in the castle's long history.

Until today, Vayn thought, with a tight smile.

Above the castle the Dragon Knights circled,

their enormous shadows sweeping across Vayn's army as both sides prepared to do battle. Vayn hated the Emperor's protectors – 'dragonbloods', born with the power to transform from men into fearsome dragons. They were legendary warriors, but their power had failed them when the Emperor and his family had had their 'tragic accident' at Vayn's hands. It had failed them when Vayn's armies had taken castle after castle across the Twelve Islands. Now only the Imperial Castle remained. Soon, the Islands of Alariss would belong to him.

Vayn sneered. *They won't trouble me any more.*

He raised his arms.

'Attack!' he bellowed.

His men bowed and crashed their armoured fists against their breastplates. The sound echoed from the castle walls. His army charged.

Ignus, the Flame Dragon, was the first of the formation to drop from the sky, meeting Vayn's men in battle. Sunlight glinted from his golden wings. Smoke trailed from his nostrils, whipping back over his crested head. His mouth opened wide, showing teeth as long as Vayn's arm and as sharp as a sword.

Fire roared from the dragon's throat, smoke billowing over the army and cutting through their ranks. Men screamed and stumbled. Even from the safety of his low hill, Vayn felt the heat.

The dragon's claws flashed out, grabbing soldiers and throwing them against the hard fortress wall. Then it was gone, lifting into the sky.

Vayn watched, emotionless, as his army charged the fortress again. He would see every one of his men die if it meant he got his hands on the throne; he could always find more men to fill his army.

A second dragon plummeted down, tucking his wings tight against his sides. Nord, the Storm Dragon, had scales as blue as a summer sky. He left a trail of freezing mist behind him as he joined the fight, and the air around him glittered with tiny frozen crystals.

A jet of icy air rushed from Nord's mouth, engulfing a group of Vayn's guards. The dragon's wings snapped back and forth, sending a cloud of mist across the battlefield. When it cleared, the guards were unmoving, frozen by the blast of arctic air. Frost had turned their black armour white.

Nord swooped over the ice-covered guards and lashed his tail into them. They shattered like glass dropped onto stone. Cheers erupted from behind the walls of the Imperial Castle.

Vayn stared at the castle with loathing. 'Cheer, you fools . . . for now.'

Ignus and Nord curved in the sky, joined now by Kyria the Water Dragon; Noctaris the Night Dragon; Taric the Mirror Dragon and Ulric the Shadow Dragon, until all six were circling above the army in a single, close formation. Magnificent wings thumped the air. Once, the sight had taken Vayn's breath away, but that was before he had begun to hate the dragons for their power and their loyalty to his brother, Emperor Marek.

Marek, also a dragonblood, had wanted to help his people, but Vayn was determined to rule with the fist. Now that he'd destroyed Marek, Vayn was ready to build a new empire in his own spiteful image.

With a cry from above, the winged knights dived.

The Black Guard faltered, raising shields and swords hopelessly above their heads.

But Vayn stayed calm, and began to chant. He might not have been born with dragonblood, unlike his precious brother, but he had learnt to wield something better. He had power – dark power.

Vayn let out a piercing cry and sent forth his powerful sorcery. A thick, black fog spread fast across the battlefield. As the dragons swept down, the fog rose to meet them. Fire, water and wind erupted from the dragons, but Vayn's magic was stronger.

Wings stopped, mid-beat. The dragons fought, but the fog was too powerful. They couldn't even flinch. Shrieking, they crashed from the sky onto the battlefield and lay motionless on the churned ground in front of the castle.

'Now!' Vayn shouted.

From behind the hill, his second army of Black Guard streamed forward to launch a renewed assault on the castle gate. Without the dragons to guard it, the gate couldn't hold. Frantic courtiers ran for their lives as the Guard overwhelmed them.

On the battlefield, guards surrounded the paralysed dragons. One by one, they clamped copper manacles around the dragons' ankles. As the manacles closed, Vayn's magic was unleashed and the dragons began to change. Scales slipped back and wings folded in, shimmering and then fading. Long tails and necks retracted. Bodies shrank. The knights' dragonforms fell away, leaving only helpless, ordinary men behind.

Vayn couldn't help himself. A cruel laugh burst from his lips. 'At last!'

He strode down to stand over one of the Dragon Knights. The man stared up at him, eyes full of hate and confusion.

'Ignus, the *Flame* Dragon,' Vayn sneered. 'Why don't you try to conjure fire now?'

A faint puff of smoke drifted across the battlefield and was gone. Vayn laughed.

Ignus's face creased with fear as he struggled against his manacles. He looked on in despair as the Imperial Castle was ransacked and people fled – some carrying babes in arms. Vayn had betrayed them all. The tendons in Ignus's neck strained as he struggled to speak. 'What have you *done*?'

Vayn stared down at the stricken Dragon Knight. Slowly, he let a smile spread across his face.

'I have taken away your power . . . '

Ignus let out cry of anguish and fury that echoed across the plain.

'Without the power of the Dragon Knights, Marek's dynasty is nothing. *Nothing!*' Vayn spat. 'Death would be too kind for the likes of you. Instead, you will come to know what it is to live in this world without dragonblood, tortured by the power you once had. I'll tell the people how the monstrous Dragon Knights murdered the Imperial Family and they will praise me for removing your menace from the land.'

He raised his voice and shoved the bound knight towards his guardsman. 'You are banished from the Imperial Isle. Take them away!'

Vayn straightened. The doors to the palace stood open. His Black Guard lined the road leading up to it and the sounds from behind the castle walls had hushed.

Vayn strode into the palace.

He was the Emperor now, the ruler of all the Islands. There was no one left who could stand against him. *No one.*

CHAPTER I

THE NEW RECRUIT

Twelve years later

Summer raged across Yaross, the most southerly island of Alariss. Birds sang in the lush green forests and colourful butterflies whirled through the warm air. The great Floating Mountains hung above the eastern slopes, shimmering pink in the hazy warmth, tendrils trailing lazily towards the ground. In the central plains, where the forest was thickest, heat rose from the ground in waves, and silver rivers slithered their way across the landscape like drowsy snakes.

Beside the timeless flow of the River Yar, a small clearing seemed to push back against the forest. Modest dwellings lined the banks on one side and pushed up against the trees on the other. Only the call of woodland birds happily going about their business could be heard – until an almighty bang nearly shook them out of the trees.

A young boy stomped out of his aunt's wooden cottage, growling with frustration. Scrawny chickens squawked and scattered out of the way of his gangly limbs.

'. . . And don't slam the door, Quinn!' a woman's voice called out.

Too late for that . . . he thought, marching across the dirt yard. The summer heat and bird-song had done nothing to put Quinn in a good mood.

'Is it my fault that the cottage is always full of wet sheets?' he muttered angrily as he strode out into the clearing in front of his home.

He kicked his way over to the woodpile by the side of the dirt road and snatched up the axe, swinging it into a length of wood. The wood split with a satisfying crack, opening like a ripe watermelon.

'Take that!' Quinn raged at being in trouble again. He did *try* to be careful, but the cottage was practically one big booby trap. He hadn't *meant* to send a whole morning's laundry crashing to the dusty floor.

He picked up another piece of wood and placed it on the block.

He was fed up with his life in the tiny village of Rivervale. His Aunt Marta – and most of the village – relied on doing work for the Black Guard; the huge Yaross Garrison was stationed just a few miles from their cottage. Without it, they would never be able to pay the taxes that Emperor Vayn demanded to protect the land from evil dragons. Apparently the Guard ensured 'peace' and 'stability' . . . although not everyone approved of their methods.

Regardless of how much work they did, though, they were still poor. Quinn's only possessions were the clothes on his back and his father's emerald-handled dagger, saved from the fishing accident that had drowned both his parents. Marta had looked after him ever since the tragedy. She used to earn money from teaching the local villagers to read or selling the odd magic potion, but the suspicious Guard soon put a stop to that – now it was laundry duty, or nothing.

Quinn took aim once more and brought the axe down, smashing the wood into kindling – sweat formed on his pale brow and slowly trickled over his amber eyes.

Lonely Yaross Island was about as far from the capital as it was possible to get without falling into the sea. No one important ever came to visit and they didn't produce anything anyone wanted. The twelve main islands had everything from the frozen glaciers of Nixia in the north, to the warm forests of Yaross in the south. Some, like The Golden Sun and The Silver Moon, had huge citadels that scraped the clouds or valuable seams of silver that brought endless wealth. Yaross had floating rocks, great mountains of them just hovering in the air with overgrown ivy trailing towards the ground.

They might be beautiful, but who wanted floating rocks?

Quinn glared at the woodpile, hefting his axe. 'It's all because of the stupid dragons . . . '

He dug his axe into the wood. For years he'd been told that the Dragon Knights were evil; that they'd sworn to protect the royal family, but had ended up betraying and killing them. Only the brave Emperor Vayn and his Black Guard had managed to save the kingdom.

His aunt might say the stories about the Dragon Knights' betrayal weren't true, but she always wanted to see the best in people. She was just making excuses, like she did for everyone.

'Two sides to every story,' she'd said. So why hadn't she been willing to listen to the other side of *his* story?

Quinn imagined the woodpile was a dragon staring back at him and he swung his axe over his head, bringing it crashing down. Splinters flew into the air. He smashed the axe into it over and over. The impact jarred the bones in his arms like he'd been whacked with an iron bar. His hands were going numb, but he didn't stop.

'Take that, dragon!' he shouted. 'And that! And that!'

The wood dragon opened its mouth. Enormous teeth like sharpened fence posts stretched towards him. Quinn slammed his axe into it, splintering the wood into tiny fragments. Sweat stuck his hair to his forehead. He hammered the dragon with his axe, harder and harder until suddenly, the dragon was gone. Quinn blinked, panting hard. The whole woodpile had been demolished.

He paused for a second to catch his breath, when suddenly, a slow hand-clap behind him broke the stillness in the air. Quinn spun round. In front of him, by the edge of his dusty yard, was a pair of creaking black leather boots. He tilted his head back. There, seated on an enormous horse that looked better fed than Quinn, was a Black Guard – and another, just behind him. They were covered from head to foot in the famous, magically strengthened black armour. It glinted in the sunlight, as hard and smooth as obsidian. Only the guards' pale, stern faces were left visible, glaring down at him. And here was Quinn, staring right back up, not showing the slightest bit of respect.

Damn it! How long have they been there? Quinn dropped to his knees and pressed his forehead into the dirt, bowing to the guards. His anger and frustration soon made way for worry – they must have thought he was a madman, slamming into the woodpile like that.

His heart hammered in his chest as he heard one of the guards dismount, and slow footsteps approach.

The boots came to a halt in front of Quinn. He flinched, expecting a kick.

'Get up,' the guard growled.

Quinn gritted his teeth and braced himself for a blow as he clambered to his feet. The guard towered over him, made to seem even bigger by the magical armour.

As if this day could get any worse . . .

'Name?' the guard barked.

'Quinn,' he replied.

'Occupation?' the other guard demanded. This voice sounded female.

'Erm . . . ' Quinn hadn't really thought about his occupation before. He occasionally went to lessons and he and Marta tried to survive day to day, but that was about it. 'Washer boy . . . I suppose. Are you here for the latest batch?' he asked hopefully.

The armoured man gave a mocking laugh. 'You think the Guard would waste time on that, boy? We have servants for that.'

'Of course,' Quinn said, relieved. Maybe he'd have a chance to put right the work he'd ruined. Although, if they weren't here for the washing . . .

The armoured man flashed a grin towards his fellow guard, his lips twisting like a vice. 'We're looking for something very different,' he snarled. 'Someone who can be of use to us . . . '

'Huh?' Quinn started.

'That was impressive – with the axe,' the guard grunted, glaring down at him. The black helmet left the lower part of his ugly face exposed. 'Wasn't it, Rowena?'

His fellow guard on the horse threw back her head and flashed her yellow teeth in a malicious grin. 'Yes, Jarin, for a weed like him.'

Quinn bristled. He was only twelve years old, but he wasn't *that* skinny.

'Though I hope that's the only dragon he's seen around these parts,' the guard continued.

'It is . . . ' Quinn replied quickly. 'I —'

'Because you would tell us, wouldn't you? If there were *dragonbloods* in your village,' the guardsman hissed, as if the mere mention of dragons was like poison in his mouth.

'Of course I would,' Quinn said, beginning to feel nervous. He'd heard the stories about what happened to people who concealed dragons. There was one boy, two villages over, who had been born with dragonblood. The villagers had tried to protect him, and they'd paid the price with their lives . . .

The guard looked him up and down, as if deciding whether or not to believe him. In the end he snorted, as if bored with the encounter. 'Perhaps you're telling the truth . . . '

Rowena gave a mocking laugh.

'. . . But that's not our purpose today.'

Quinn was confused. He was used to being ignored by the Black Guard. The only times he'd been this close before he'd been cuffed out of the way.

Jarin pushed back his cloak. An enormous, curved sword jutted from his belt. Quinn's breath caught and his mouth turned dry. That sword could take his head right off his neck.

The guardsman reached into a pocket tied to his belt and pulled out a scroll. He threw it at Quinn who caught it instinctively.

'The Guard needs new blood.' The man loomed over him. 'And since you've got nothing better to do than hack away at a wooden dragon . . . '

Quinn stared up at him. 'What are you talking about?'

The guard swung back up onto his horse. 'Welcome to the Black Guard, trainee.'

'Good luck,' Rowena sneered, as she spurred her horse. 'A worm like you is going to need it.'

CHAPTER 2

THE HIDDEN TRUTH

The next morning Quinn rolled out of bed, groaning.

Every muscle in his body ached. His shoulders were so stiff he could hardly lift his arms. It felt as though one of the Floating Mountains had come crashing down in the night and flattened him. His hands were covered in blisters from where he'd swung his axe too hard.

He pushed his dark hair away from his face and rubbed his eyes, feeling the early morning light wash over him. Suddenly the thought was upon him again: *I'm being enrolled in the Guard.*

He reached into his shirt and pulled out the scroll the guard had thrown to him. He'd slept on it in the night and it had crumpled, but he recognised the seal of the Imperial Castle and Vayn's flag with its black fist. No one would *dare* copy that.

Quinn's fingers trembled as he levered off the seal and unrolled the scroll once again:

To the Commanders of the Twelve Garrisons of the Islands,
His Imperial Highness, the Emperor Vayn, Ruler of Alariss, hereby commands all garrisons to recruit new forces. The Black Guard must be strengthened to ensure peace in our lands. The dragonblood menace must not be allowed to return!

Below the message from the Emperor, in a different hand, a word from local Guard Leader Goric – well known and despised – summoned the recipient of the command to the Yaross Garrison.

It was real. Quinn was going to be a Black Guard trainee, one of the Emperor's elite, defending the realm just like he'd imagined. He would get the magical black armour and a real sword and travel the Twelve Islands from Nixia to Yaross.

It *was* true that a lot of the guards Quinn had met were cruel bullies, and he'd heard some terrible stories about them whispered around the village. He knew first-hand about Goric and his quick fists – but *he* wouldn't be like that. He wouldn't treat ordinary people like dirt. He'd be working for the good of the Islands and the Emperor. And besides . . . who wanted to be a washer boy for the rest of their life?

But now he realised that he would have to tell Aunt Marta, and a wave of sickness came over him. He'd avoided telling her the night before – the argument about the sheets had still hung in the air like a dark cloud – but he couldn't delay any longer. Quinn was all she had, and he was supposed to report to the garrison that morning.

He straightened up, forgetting his aches, and

pulled aside the heavy curtain that separated his corner of the cottage from the living area.

Marta was already up, hunched over a sheet in the firelight, neatly darning a hole in one of Quinn's socks. She looked peaceful and calm, her greying hair bunched up on top of her head.

She smiled up at him, all traces of yesterday's argument gone. 'You're up early.'

Quinn grinned weakly. 'I couldn't sleep.'

'Well then, have some breakfast, nephew.'

'I-I have something you need to see . . . ' he stuttered.

'After you eat, Quinn,' Marta replied.

'No, Aunt. Now.' He fumbled in his shirt and pulled out the scroll.

Marta took it, frowning, and unrolled it in the light from the fire. As she slowly read the words, the colour drained from her face. She turned to Quinn, wide-eyed, desperate-looking, and clutched his arm weakly.

'No . . . '

Quinn stared back at her. *No?* How could she just say no?

'I have to. The guards . . . It's not a question, it's an order!' Quinn exclaimed, grabbing back the scroll and stuffing it into his shirt.

'No! I can't allow it!' Marta cried, with a note of terror in her voice.

Quinn took a step back. 'But I thought you might be pleased. No more laundry work, no more darning sheets. We don't have to be poor any more!'

She shook her head, tears welling in her eyes. 'I care nothing for riches!'

'Well I care nothing for sheets!' he argued. 'I can't stay here forever!'

His aunt just stared at him through teary eyes. 'I know that, Nephew,' she started. 'But there's so much you don't know. So much you don't understand. I wanted to wait until you were older – I didn't want to burden you with this yet . . . '

'What are you talking about?'

Marta looked like she'd aged twenty years. He'd always known his aunt was old, but she'd never *looked* it. Not until now. She looked . . . scared.

'. . . Now I have no choice.' She looked up at Quinn, who was already a head taller than her, and sighed. 'The things you've been taught about dragons are wrong.'

Quinn's shoulders slumped. 'Not this again.' She was always hinting that the Dragon Knights weren't so bad, but whenever he asked what she meant, she just shook her head. He loved his aunt, but he just didn't get it.

'Everyone knows what the Dragon Knights did. They killed the Emperor, one of their dragon-blood. They betrayed the kingdom.'

Marta sank back and shook her head. 'I wasn't always a washerwoman, you know. I didn't always live on Yaross Island.'

That got Quinn's attention. He frowned. 'You didn't?' Surely she'd always been here, in this muddy hut, scrubbing away at sheets. But then, his parents hadn't been from Yaross Island, so maybe Marta wasn't either.

'I was a high-born lady,' Marta said.

'You?' He stared, then blushed, realising how rude he sounded. 'Sorry.'

She shook her head. 'It's fine. It's good. You weren't supposed to know – it was safer that way. I was one of the old Empress Isaria's ladies-in-waiting.' She smiled, staring into the fire. 'I lived in the Imperial Castle in the time of the Dragon Knights. I knew some of them. The Empress was like a sister to me.'

Quinn's mouth hung open. 'You *knew* them? But . . . the Dragon Knights were *evil*.'

'Haven't I told you not to trust what the Black Guard say, Quinn?' Marta frowned. 'Why trust the people who oppress us?'

Quinn began to feel like the floor was shifting from under him – like things weren't as certain as he'd once believed.

'But wasn't it worse before . . . in the old days with the dragons?'

Marta plucked a pinch of dust from the floor of the hut, then lifted it to her lips and whispered something. Quinn felt the familiar tingle of magic. Marta tossed the dust into the fire.

'Watch . . . and learn the truth.'

The flames reared up in the small fireplace,

twisting and splitting apart. Quinn stared at them. Through the magic smoke an image formed of a gigantic castle perched on a low hill. Great sloping stone walls reached high into the sky. Behind them stood a palace with thirteen enormous angular towers, one for each of the main islands and a tall, central tower, for the Imperial Family.

'Is that the Imperial Castle?' Quinn asked. He'd only ever imagined it. But he hadn't dreamed it would be so *big*. You could drop the whole of his village into it and it would be lost in that place.

His aunt nodded.

Above the castle, in the flames, vast dragons circled ominously.

Quinn stared at them, his heart racing. They were even more terrifying than he'd imagined.

'They're attacking the castle,' Quinn said. 'I said they were evil. How can you defend them?'

'Watch,' his aunt said again.

The great shapes of the dragons were just below him. If he reached towards the fire, he would be able to touch them. Brightly coloured scales glittered. Muscles bunched and stretched beneath the skin. Just seeing how powerful they were made Quinn shiver.

Beneath the dragons stood the Black Guard. He couldn't even count how many of them there were.

'What's happening?' Quinn whispered. He thought the Black Guard were supposed to be on the same side as the Imperial Guard. *What were they doing outside the castle?*

The red dragon below Quinn roared, and fire billowed from its mouth.

'We are the last line of defence.' The red dragon's voice echoed through Marta's magic, distant but clear. 'All others have fallen. There is nowhere else to retreat. We swore our lives to this. Now is the time to fulfil that oath. Defend the castle!'

As the army of Black Guard below began its charge, the red dragon dropped towards them.

Quinn watched in growing confusion as, one by one, the dragons launched attacks against the Black Guard, then, as the fog rose around them, the dragons fell.

This wasn't the way it had been told to him. The dragons had been the ones who murdered the Emperor and his family. That's what everyone had said. Yet here was the Black Guard attacking the castle.

Quinn saw the dragons brought down and what looked like a metal bracelet being clamped onto their ankles. Then he saw Vayn stride into the palace and proclaim himself Emperor.

The flames died away.

'The manacles,' Quinn gawped. 'So, that's what it is to be bound . . . '

'Yes,' Marta explained. 'They trap the Dragon Knights in their human form.'

'So they can't harm anyone?'

'So they can't harm *Vayn*,' Marta continued. 'Vayn murdered the Emperor and Empress and other high-born people – heirs – too. He blamed the Dragon Knights. He exiled them.'

Quinn looked down at the scroll in disbelief. The Black Guard were the traitors. *They* were the murderers, not the Dragon Knights. All their bullying and stealing wasn't to protect the Islands. They were just thieves.

Now he was supposed to become one of them and swear allegiance to Vayn, the man who had murdered his own brother to become Emperor?

He couldn't do it. Everything he had been taught had turned out to be false and now he knew the truth.

And the truth changed everything . . .

CHAPTER 3

AN UNWELCOME VISITOR

'What am I going to do?' Quinn cried, staring blankly at Marta. He was supposed to report to the barracks this morning but he couldn't go and join the Black Guard. Not now he knew that they were liars and that Emperor Vayn had stolen the throne. 'Why didn't you tell me?'

'I couldn't put you in danger. Knowledge is a powerful thing in Alariss,' his aunt said. 'There is no other option, now. We must run!' she cried. She grabbed a bag and began shoving things into it. 'I brought you here to the farthest of the Islands to get you away from the Black

Guard. You have been safe for twelve years and I will not let them have you now. Get everything you need. We must leave within the hour.'

Quinn scrambled up, his heart pounding. Yesterday, all he'd been worried about was being in trouble for knocking over the laundry. Today, he had to run away from everything he'd ever known.

He snatched up a bag and headed for his corner of the cottage. He rummaged through his few possessions and bundled in some clothes. Suddenly he remembered his father's knife, the only thing of value that had been left to him, and rushed to the high shelf where he kept it safe.

'Quinn, wait!' Marta cried out, before he had a chance to grab it. 'There's something else I have to tell you. Something important. You —'

Before she could finish, a loud thumping sounded from the door, and a harsh voice shouted out:

'Open up, in the name of the Emperor!'

Quinn froze. It had to be the Black Guard.

'We have to go – *now!*' he hissed.

Behind him, Marta put her finger to her lips and urged Quinn to be quiet. She picked up a handful of dust from the floor and whispered into it once more, muttering a barring spell. Slowly, magic pulsed its way through the air, pushing against the door like a pair of invisible hands.

'Go!' Marta said under her breath. 'I'll hold them off.'

Quinn started for the back door, but just then something came crashing into their home. Hinges splintered and the barring spell shattered. Marta stumbled back as an enormous armoured figure strode in, his head brushing against the top of the wooden doorway.

Quinn shot a look at the back door. Even if he could reach it, there were bound to be other guards outside their home. He'd have to make for the forest, or maybe the river – but either one would involve crossing half the village. He was fast, but didn't know if he was that fast, and the guards' swords were very long and very sharp.

Marta shook her head, as though she knew what Quinn was thinking.

Slowly, the guard looked from their half-packed bags, to the scroll lying by the fireplace, to Quinn's stricken face. How could this look like anything other than what it was? It couldn't have been any more obvious that they were about to flee if he'd scribbled it on a sign and hung it around his neck.

Marta dropped to the ground and bowed before the guard. Quinn copied her.

'What have we done to receive the honour of your visit, Goric?' Marta asked courteously, her words muffled by the floor. Quinn knew his aunt well enough to recognise the tremble in her voice. She was afraid, and with good reason. Goric was the captain of the Black Guard on Yaross Island. Compared to Goric, the guards Quinn had met the day before were just irritating fleas.

'Why did you bar your door with magic,

Marta?' Goric said, coldly. 'Does the name of the Emperor mean nothing to you? Do you plan treason?'

Quinn shuddered. Goric would do anything to make life difficult for him and Marta. Once, when Quinn was just a baby, Goric had wanted to marry Marta, but she had turned him down. He had held a grudge ever since. Looking at the brutal man with the curling lip, cold blue eyes and icy pale skin, Quinn shuddered to imagine him being part of their family. Goric had never hesitated to use those great big fists on any of the villagers who irritated him.

'No, Goric,' Marta whispered. 'We honour the Emperor.'

'Honour,' Goric hissed. 'You have no honour.' He tore down a line of damp laundry that stretched across the middle of the hut. 'You never did. But today I have come to teach you about honour. When my men told me they'd recruited your nephew, I thought I'd do you the *honour* of collecting him myself.' He stamped over to where Quinn still knelt, head pressed against the ground. All Quinn could see were the big boots and the shiny black armour above. 'After all, we wouldn't want any *accident* to befall him that would prevent him making it to the garrison.'

Quinn shivered. Goric made it sound like a threat. He had been waiting for years to get revenge on Marta. This was just the excuse he'd been looking for.

To think Quinn had imagined joining the Black Guard trainees might be a great adventure – now he knew it was going to be a nightmare.

His hands trembled where he clutched at the floor. He was having trouble breathing.

Then, he felt something strange wash over him – Marta's magic! It slowed his pulse and calmed his breathing. He felt able to think more clearly. He glanced across at her. She smiled, and suddenly he felt something heavy materialise in his pocket. Marta had transported something there! His eyes widened. Marta nodded, and mouthed, 'Ready?'

Ready? He wanted to say. *Ready for what?*

But he didn't have time. Marta leapt to her feet and her magic surged. Quinn felt it lash out like a whip. The magic pulsed out from Marta in colourful rays, like nothing Quinn had seen before. She'd always had so little magic – or seemed to. It was as if it had all been saved up for this one moment.

Goric staggered – his armour was far too strong for the magic, but that didn't mean he wasn't caught off balance by its powerful blast. He tumbled backwards, clutching on to the wet sheets that hung above him, pulling them down as he crashed to the floor. The glasses and plates in the cottage shattered, sending shards slicing through the air. The floor shook with energy. This was Quinn's moment; his aunt was giving him a chance.

'Now!' Marta yelled to Quinn. 'Run!'

CHAPTER 4

UP IN FLAMES

Quinn hit the back door with his shoulder and barged it open. He stumbled through, put his head down and ran.

Behind him, he heard Goric roar in anger and something smash inside the cottage as he took out his fury on their furniture. If Quinn could get to the forest, he could hide and he would be safe. The Guard wouldn't chase him in; it was too tangled and dark, and everyone knew there were things in there that you didn't want to mess with. Then he could go back for Marta.

The door smashed off its hinges behind Quinn, and Goric pushed his way out.

'Stop him!' the Captain of the Guard yelled.

Quinn couldn't let that happen. He sprinted across the yard, legs pumping. He pushed his hair away from his eyes to clear his sight, and only just in time. One of the guards loomed up in front of him. Quinn darted around him, but his foot slipped and he almost fell. He pushed himself up and ran on.

Just another hundred yards, he thought, *and I'll be free!*

He put on a burst of speed.

Quinn saw two enormous black figures step out from behind a neighbouring house. He tried to dodge them, but he was running too fast. One of the guards caught him by his arm, spun him around and threw him to the ground. The breath exploded out of Quinn's chest. His head swam as his skull bounced off the hard earth, dirt clouding his vision.

Before he could even blink his eyes clear, the guard had hauled him up. Quinn struggled, but the other guard smacked him around the head. Quinn felt suddenly sick.

'Stop struggling or I'll do more than bruise your head,' the guard growled.

Quinn let out a cry as the first guard twisted his arm behind his back. He recognised him as Jarin, the one who'd mocked him the day before.

The other guard grabbed his arm – *Rowena*. Together, they dragged him back to the cottage. As they reached it, Quinn saw Goric emerge. The captain's face was still red with anger, and he was hauling Marta behind him like a sack of turnips. She looked only half conscious.

'Let her go!' Quinn shouted. Goric's black metal gauntlet squeezed her thin arm so tight Quinn was sure he was going to break it.

'As you wish, Quinn,' Goric smirked, as he threw Marta down on the ground. She landed loosely and Quinn winced. Goric turned to his guards with a cruel laugh. 'Burn the house!'

'NO!' Quinn yelled. He struggled with the guards, but they were too strong.

Rowena left Jarin to hold Quinn back and

grabbed a thick branch from the woodpile. She dashed into the house and returned with the branch aflame, lit from Marta's own fire. She flashed Quinn a sinister grin, then tossed the torch onto the thatched roof. Quinn watched as the flames caught and the dry straw started to crackle. He threw himself forward, but Jarin jerked him back. He saw the fire leap across the roof as though it were alive, and there was nothing he could do about it.

Everything they had was in there. Quinn knew that they'd never had much, just a few clothes and some old wooden toys, but it was all in there. Marta's belongings, too: her one good dress from long ago, magic ingredients and her neat pile of yellowing letters and writing tools.

He wrenched at the guard's grip, but the man was twice his size. Jarin laughed as the flames twisted up and Quinn stared at him furiously. His breath came hot and fast. They couldn't do this to Marta! It was her whole life! Quinn had watched Marta working so *hard* cleaning the guards' clothes and sheets every day of her life and now they were burning her house. *How dare they do this to her?* he thought. Anger bubbled up in him, far more intense than when he'd hacked at the woodpile. Then he'd just been angry. Now he was furious. His skin flushed, and he felt scalding hot all over, like the rage was burning him up, like fire was creeping over his skin,

The guardsman holding him yelped and snatched his hand away, looking at it in surprise.

'A spark from the burning cottage,' he muttered. 'It must have been . . .'

Quinn didn't wait for the man to grab him again. He lunged forward, past the guards to where Marta lay near the cottage. It was all burning now. Quinn knew there was no way he could save it. He could see the walls cracking with the heat and the wooden door smouldering. Inside, the flames had found their way to Marta's laundry. Quinn saw it blazing like a furnace. Marta was so close to the fire, even her clothes were starting to char. Quinn grabbed her and pulled her back. He was so angry he didn't even notice the heat.

Quinn glared at Goric with fury as he pulled his aunt to safety. He knew he should be bowing and stammering apologies to the Captain of the Guard, but he couldn't. Goric hadn't had to do any of this. Quinn would have gone to be a trainee to protect his aunt, but Goric was *enjoying* this. He was laughing.

'The cottage can be rebuilt,' Goric said. 'But next time you defy me, *boy*, your aunt will be inside it when I burn it down.' He swung up onto his horse, gathering the reins in one hand. 'Take the boy to the garrison for training,' he told the others. He kicked his horse viciously and set off ahead of them.

Marta stirred and coughed weakly. To Quinn, her face looked red from the heat of the fire, and there was a smear of blood under her nose. She reached up with thin, trembling arms and hugged him. Quinn blinked away tears.

'Don't worry,' Marta whispered. 'I'll go into exile. He won't be able to hurt me any more, and he won't be able to use me to threaten you. You'll be all right.'

Quinn felt his throat choking up. 'What am I going to do?'

She stroked his cheek and smiled. 'Stay safe. Do what Goric tells you. Keep out of trouble, but stay true to your heart. I'll come for you as soon as I can, I promise. This won't last forever.'

'Enough!' Rowena growled, stalking over to them. She grabbed Quinn's arm and jerked him up. Marta slumped back to the ground. 'Come with me. You're one of us now.'

Quinn turned his head to stare at the blackened remains of his home as the guards dragged him away.

I might have to be a trainee, he thought, *but I'll never be one of you. Never.*

CHAPTER 5

THE GARRISON

They had been riding for hours by the time they came in sight of the garrison and despite the sunshine dipping through the trees, Quinn felt a dark cloud of despair hanging over him. He'd clung on to Jarin in a daze as the horse clipped through the forest, Rowena and Goric travelling up ahead. Every time the horse had taken a step, Quinn's backside had thumped on the hard saddle and the jolt had travelled all the way up his back to clatter his teeth. He could actually *feel* the purple bruises forming with each whack of the saddle – though it was nothing compared to the pain of seeing his house burned to the ground or the look on Aunt Marta's face.

The garrison's outer gate was a massive, stone construction at least four storeys high. Two round towers flanked the enormous gateway, with arrow slits piercing the stonework every couple of yards. A heavy iron portcullis hung above the gate. As he rode beneath it, Quinn peered up at it with a shudder. If it dropped, he and the horse would both be squashed flatter than one of Marta's pancakes.

At least I wouldn't have to be in the Guard, he thought darkly.

The courtyard in front of him was almost as big as Quinn's village. To the left, straw targets in the shape of huge dragons had been set up. Quinn watched as the guards fired arrow after arrow into them. To the right, he saw a group of trainees a year or two older than him battering at each other with wooden swords. Nerves crept across him like vines across the forest floor, but he held them in check. He wouldn't let the Guard get to him.

Abruptly, the horse came to a stop. Jarin gave him a little push to 'help' him, and Quinn cried out as he slid off into the dirt.

'Hey!' he shouted.

'Stop moaning,' Goric snapped, as he dismounted his own huge mare. 'You're in the Black Guard now. You'd better get used to being uncomfortable.'

Does that mean lying in the dirt? Quinn thought, ignoring Goric. He gazed up at the garrison building. It might have seemed like prison – and he was sure it would be like hell for the recruits – but it was the grandest prison he'd ever imagined. The building in front of him was at least a hundred yards long and two storeys high. Half a dozen narrow towers jutted above the building flying the flag of the Twelve Islands: a clenched black fist on a red background that made Quinn shiver.

And it's made of stone, he thought. *It's not bad for some.* Builders on Yaross had a hard time coaxing the levitating rocks from the Floating Mountains into submission: material that stayed on the ground didn't come cheap.

'New recruits must report to the main garrison . . . ' Goric barked.

Quinn trudged across the courtyard, the mid-afternoon heat rising from the ground in waves. He caught the smells drifting out of the kitchen and his stomach clenched. *Bacon*, he thought, his mouth watering. *And freshly baked bread.* All he and Marta had had last night were summer fruits and nuts. He started to wonder where the dragon-fighting taxes really went.

At the thought of Marta, he felt for the package in his pocket. He wondered what had been so important that she'd had to use magic to get it to him without the Black Guard noticing. He had to find somewhere quiet before he could take a look.

'You're not sightseeing!' Rowena barked. 'Follow me and tie up that horse!'

Quinn jumped. Too busy daydreaming, he'd almost forgotten he was standing in the middle of the courtyard. He walked back, grabbed hold of the horse's bridle and pulled it after Rowena, tying it up in the huge stables.

'You, boy!' a harsh voice shouted.

Quinn looked around and saw that another, smaller guard was striding towards him, black armour glinting in the afternoon sun. The raised black fist embossed on the breastplate of the armour seemed to be aimed right at him. Quinn couldn't help flinching.

'Your papers,' the guard demanded. 'Do you think I've got time to hang about all day?'

Quinn pulled the scroll from inside his shirt,

Taking care to conceal Marta's package, Quinn pulled the scroll from inside his shirt and held it before him. The guard snatched it up.

The summer sun was hot on Quinn's back and the dust from the courtyard got in his mouth and nose and eyes. His mouth felt like a dry well, desperate for a drop of rain.

The guard stiffened in front of him. Quinn's heart stuttered. *Did he see Marta's package inside my jacket?*

Nervously, he looked up at the guard, but noticed that he wasn't even looking at him.

Instead, he was staring away over Quinn's back, as though he'd completely forgotten that he existed. Quinn shuffled carefully around. All he could see were hooves as yet more mounted guards rode into the courtyard.

The first horse snorted and abruptly came to a halt. A moment later, Quinn saw a golden boot swing down to land with a puff of dust on the courtyard. Something was different about this guard. Around him, trainee and guardsman alike dropped into a bow.

Quinn saw a line of golden medals pinned to the man's smart, night-blue military jacket. He wasn't wearing the black armour of the Guard, Quinn saw, but the Guard seemed wary of him.

The only people who wear clothes like that are the Emperor's courtiers, Quinn thought, as he peered at the man. *But they never come this far south . . .*

He shifted his head so he could get a better look. The man was tall and thin, with deep-set eyes. He glanced around haughtily, like he owned the place. Behind him, on the ground, Quinn spotted what looked like a ragged heap tied up behind the man's saddle.

Goric strode forward to greet him.

'Marshall Stant. Welcome to Yaross Island. We didn't expect you so early.'

Stant! Quinn recognised that name. The man was notoriously cruel. The Emperor used him to put down rebellions. He was the one who would destroy villages harbouring those with dragonblood.

Stant peered slowly around the courtyard. 'So I see,' he said. His voice was as cold as his eyes.

'Untie her!' Goric commanded.

Quinn watched several of Goric's guards leap to their feet and hurry over to the marshall's horse. Now Quinn could see that the shape tied to the back of Stant's horse wasn't just a bunch of rags, it was a girl.

Another recruit, Quinn thought. *At least I got to ride* on *the horse.*

Quinn could barely make out what she looked like. She was covered in dust and mud from head to toe, and she was bleeding and scraped in a dozen places. She was clutching her left arm tight to her body as though it was broken. Quinn noticed the enormous bruise on the side of her face.

The girl let out a moan as the guards untied her roughly and shoved her back down to the ground. Quinn tensed. Couldn't they see she was hurt?

Stant laughed. 'The girl's been causing trouble,' he called. He turned slowly to eye the trainees. Quinn avoided the gaze. 'This is what happens when you cause trouble . . .'

Goric laughed heartily. 'True enough, Stant. Although why we need such a useless girl —'

Rowena spluttered.

Quinn knew that female officers in the Black Guard were rare, but that didn't mean they weren't just as fearsome as the men. Emperor Vayn was the friend of anyone who shared his cruel outlook – Rowena clearly demonstrated that.

'What I mean is,' Goric continued, avoiding Rowena's glare, 'why not put an end to her if she has caused such problems?'

Quinn flinched at Goric's brutality.

Marshall Stant turned his cold eyes on Captain Goric. 'It is not for you to question, Goric. The decision does not belong with a mere captain of Yaross Island, it goes much higher than that.'

Goric looked taken aback and tried to stutter a reply, but he was completely lost for words. Quinn caught the girl's flashing green eyes that seemed to smile in his direction. He had to stifle a grin. For the first time in years he'd seen Goric humiliated. It was worth a laugh whether he was stuck in the Black Guard garrison or not.

Suddenly the mood darkened once more. 'Enough of this,' Stant cried. 'Lock the girl up in your dungeon.'

The dungeon? Couldn't they see the state she was in? She needed help. A guardsman grabbed the girl by her injured arm and started to drag her towards the garrison building. She let out a scream of pain and her eyes seemed to plead with Quinn.

'Stop!' Quinn shouted instinctively, as he leapt to his feet.

The whole courtyard fell silent and turned to look at him. Quinn's hand shot to his mouth. Marta had told him to keep out of trouble, but he'd only been at the garrison for ten minutes and already he was diving into it headfirst. It was just the same with the washing hanging up in their cottage; he couldn't seem to avoid it.

Marshall Stant looked at him in disgust. Quickly, he threw himself down to the ground and bowed again. Goric stamped over. He drew his sword and planted his boot on the back of Quinn's neck, pinning him to the ground. Quinn squirmed in fear.

'Shall I kill him for his disrespect?' Goric called, desperate to regain Stant's approval. 'We haven't started training him yet. It will be no loss.'

Quinn grimaced. Goric's boot was twisting his neck so painfully it felt like it was going to break.

'No,' Marshall Stant said, slowly. 'I have a better idea. If this *boy* values Thea's life so much, why don't we give him the chance to earn it? Let's see what he's made of.'

Marshall Stant looked around at the rest of the trainees who were still crouched unmoving, heads pressed into the dirt of the courtyard. Stant pointed a gloved hand to the largest of the trainees, a great hulking boy named Jori, almost the size of a grown-up with muscles that would have made a bull jealous.

'The boy can fight this trainee. If he wins, Thea will be treated well and join the other trainees. If he loses,' – for the first time, Stant smiled – 'they will both be put to death, here, today.'

Quinn gulped.

Stay out of trouble? This wasn't what Marta had had in mind.

CHAPTER 6

THE FIRST FIGHT

The guards and the trainees formed a circle in the centre of the courtyard. Before Quinn could react, one of the guards had shoved him right into the middle of it. He stumbled to his knees and looked up.

The hulking trainee Stant had picked out was watching him with a grin on his great flat face. He flexed his fists. Muscles rippled across his body.

'We fight until one of us can't get up,' Jori growled. 'Those are the only rules.'

Quinn swallowed hard. The trainee looked

like he could rip him apart with his bare hands, then pick up the pieces and squeeze them into sausages. That was if he didn't just pound Quinn into the courtyard dirt first.

Jori bent and tossed something to Quinn.

'Here,' he barked, with a smug smile forming in the corner of his mouth. 'Take this.'

It hit the ground by Quinn's feet with a clank. Quinn bent over and peered at it. It was a length of chain about as long as his outstretched arms, with flat weights at each end. He looked at it, puzzled.

'That's your weapon,' said Jori.

Quinn frowned. 'You're kidding. What even is this . . . ?' But before he had a chance to work it out, Goric's voice barked out behind him.

'Fight!'

The guards and trainees pushed in closer, forming a solid, jeering circle around both Quinn and Jori. Quinn knew he couldn't escape if he wanted to.

Jori picked up another chain and began spinning it around his head with one hand. Quinn barely managed to grab his own before the trainee was on to him. Jori's other hand came up, grabbed the middle of his chain, and whipped it right at Quinn.

Quinn flicked his head to one side, but not quickly enough. The weight on the end of the chain grazed the edge of his forehead. He stumbled back.

'Too slow!' Jori smirked. 'This is going to be easy.'

Quinn tried swinging his own chain at the trainee. It was heavy and far more difficult than it looked. The trainee stepped easily out of reach and Quinn ended up whacking himself on the knee as the chain swung back his way. He winced as it cracked against the bone.

Goric laughed. 'You should have waited longer to cause trouble,' he called. 'Trainees don't start learning the chain until they've been here at least a day.'

We'll see about causing trouble, Quinn thought.

Jori swung his chain again and Quinn crouched, watching him. *Maybe if he misses and I strike back quickly . . .*

The chain snapped out. Quinn tried to block it with his own, but it was no good. It smacked into his stomach, knocking him back. He sprawled in the dirt, gasping for breath. His chest felt like it was on fire. He could hear the laughter of the guards carrying across the courtyard. The trainee circled him again, twirling the chain.

Get up! Get up!

Quinn scrambled to his feet, still feeling dizzy and fighting against the pain and the lack of air. One of the guards stepped in from the circle and shoved Quinn forward. He stumbled towards Jori. The trainee's weighted chain caught him on the side of the head again, and he tumbled back to the ground. Blood flowed down over his ear.

Quinn realised it was no use. The trainee was too big and too strong. His arms were almost twice as long as Quinn's. Quinn knew he was never going to beat the older boy with brute strength. Instead, he'd have to rely on the only muscle that really counts: the brain.

He staggered to his feet, watching the trainee. The bigger boy was sweating in the heat. He was heavy and slow – he'd be quick to tire. Quinn was fast and agile – if he had any hope he'd have to use that to his advantage to out-manoeuvre his opponent.

Jori swung again, but this time Quinn was ready. He didn't try to use his own chain. He twisted on the ground and leapt back as Jori's chain whistled past.

The crowd jeered.

'Fight him!' Goric shouted. 'Fight him, you coward!'

Quinn didn't listen. Instead, he kept on dodging, retreating, moving left then right, ducking and diving.

With a roar of frustration, the trainee lashed out his chain again and again. Ignoring the pain and the blood flowing down the side of his face, Quinn kept light on his feet. Jori became more and more frustrated. He swung his chain in every direction.

Quinn smiled inwardly. *It's working!*

'Stay still!' Jori shouted. His face had turned red. 'Get back here!'

The crowd booed and shouted, but the trainee was slowing down. His attacks were becoming wilder. Sweat had soaked his shirt. Quinn saw how the boy was struggling to raise his chain.

'Kill him!' Goric yelled at Jori. 'Rip his head off!'

Jori charged, flailing with the chain. As he stumbled past, Quinn whacked his own chain across the trainee's back. The bigger boy stumbled, and the crowd went silent, sensing the change in fortunes.

Quinn backed up again. He could see his opponent was exhausted; his eyes were full of fury. Quinn remembered something his aunt had told him once when she'd patched him up after a fight in the village: *if you get angry, you lose.* He took a calming breath and watched the trainee. Then he let himself smile.

'Come at me . . . '

Quinn's smug smile drove the trainee crazy, just as Quinn had hoped. Jori's eyes widened.

61

His face flushed red. Then he threw himself at Quinn, forgetting all about the chain.

The chain was too difficult a weapon. It would take weeks, maybe even months, for Quinn to figure out how to use it properly. So instead, he had to improvise. He let it fall through his hands, then gripped tight on the heavy metal weight at one end of the chain. As the trainee charged towards him like an enraged bull, Quinn swung the weight and simply threw it at the trainee. It left his hand and flew through the air, smacking right into the trainee's head. Quinn saw Jori's eyes roll up and his knees buckle. Then he crashed into Quinn and they both tumbled to the floor. The crowd around them gasped.

With a grunt, Quinn pushed the trainee's limp weight off him. The boy was out cold and the crowd was deathly silent.

Quinn's head was still ringing from the earlier blow, and being knocked flying to the ground with the enormous trainee on top of him hadn't helped. His stomach ached as if he'd been kicked by a horse. He rocked back on his heels, gulping for air.

Did I win? he wondered.

He peered around at the crowd. They were staring at him in silence, mouths hanging open in shock. Not a single one of them had expected him to beat Jori. Quinn felt a little surge of anger. They'd all expected him to be killed.

Marshall Stant raised a hand and Quinn immediately fell into a bow. He knew now was *not* the time to irritate the marshall any more. Quinn was still bowing when a noise like a whip crack sounded above him. He braced himself for the blow, but it never came. With a shiver, he looked up. As he raised his head, something warm and wet ran over his hands. It was Jori's blood.

'Stand!' the marshall growled.

Quinn jumped to his feet. His hands were still shaking. When he clenched them, he could still feel the other trainee's blood. He stared at Marshall Stant's intricately patterned night-blue jacket and the line of golden medals.

The marshall's hard eyes burned into Quinn's face. 'You have impressed me, boy,' he said in his low, rough voice. 'You thought quickly and used your strengths. You will make a fine addition to the Black Guard.'

'If you say so . . . ' Quinn panted, determined never to be one of them.

Stant leaned in closer to Quinn, until he could feel the hot, sour breath of the marshall on his face. 'But the next time you speak out of turn, boy, I will cut out your tongue.'

Quinn stared blankly. He might have impressed Stant, but life at the garrison had just got a lot more deadly.

CHAPTER 7

A MAGIC TOUCH

Every evening, when night fell across Yaross, dinner was served in the garrison's Great Hall.

Guards hustled Quinn and the other new recruits inside and pushed them through a long, low corridor. The other recruits had wanted nothing to do with Quinn after he'd defeated Jori, and he'd spent most of the last two days dodging their suspicious glances and snide comments. Eating alone, training alone, sleeping alone in a corner of the Great Hall; he couldn't tell if they hated him or feared him. They still managed to ignore him when he was in the centre of the jostling crowd. They were acting like he had an infectious disease.

Fine, let them ignore me, Quinn thought wearily, growing used to being the lone trainee.

Quinn shrugged them off and made his way into the hall. It was a sight he'd never get used to. The Great Hall was huge. The floor was paved with flagstones and covered in fresh rushes. A great beamed ceiling stretched high above, decorated with banners and swords. Against one wall a spit turned inside an enormous fireplace and the whole vast room smelled of woodsmoke and spices. At the far end of the hall, a high table stretched almost the width of the room. Behind it, a gigantic tapestry showed a scene of the Black Guard defending the Imperial Castle against the attacking Dragon Knights.

Something else he'd never get used to. *A lie!* Quinn raged.

As ever, Quinn forced down his revulsion and kept his expression blank. He couldn't risk irritating the guards again – not if he wanted to keep his tongue. Only a few days ago he'd thought the Dragon Knights were evil, but now he knew the truth – Marta had shown him what had really happened when Emperor Vayn had taken over.

The guards' tables were groaning with food. A whole roast pig lay along the high table, with an apple stuffed into its mouth. Heaps of roast and boiled vegetables steamed on platters. There was fresh bread in piles, along with fish, cheese and full flagons of wine.

Quinn's mouth watered as he made his way over to the serving hatch – but he wasn't expecting fine dining.

'Grub's up!' the cook barked, as he thrust a steaming bowl of something into Quinn's hands.

Quinn looked down at the watery soup and what looked like yesterday's bread floating in the middle like a stranded ship.

'Great,' he muttered.

The cook just looked at him like he was something that had been scraped off the ground, and barked at the next recruit to come forward.

Quinn headed for one of the benches. Normally

he'd eat alone, but just as he was about to barge a path through the crowd of recruits to a quiet table, he spotted a better prospect: the girl from the courtyard.

Now that she was cleaned up, he almost didn't recognise her – it was only the flashing green eyes that gave her away. She had red hair and pale skin with freckles across her cheeks. Her clothing might have been torn and scraped from being pulled behind Stant's horse, but to Quinn it looked far more expensive than anything he'd ever worn. She beckoned to him and a smile played across Quinn's face. He made for the table in a quiet corner of the room and slid in beside her. She still looked bruised and battered, and her broken arm was obviously still hurting her.

'You made it out of the dungeon, then?' Quinn smiled. 'Marshall Stant said he'd release you, but he's not to be trusted.'

'I had to bribe my way out with my necklace.' She grinned. 'The guards are just as crooked as they look.'

'I don't doubt it. I'm Quinn, by the way.'

'Thea,' she said. 'Hi.'

Quinn looked around at the recruits as they dug into their meals. Most of them were boys, and most of them were about Quinn's age, but there were some girls too. The guards would happily take anyone who could swing an axe and turn them into one of Vayn's hate-filled minions.

'Thanks, by the way,' Thea said.

Quinn tentatively poked at the bread floating in his soup. 'What for?'

'You know.' She nodded at her broken arm. 'For helping me.'

Quinn just nodded, sheepishly.

'Seriously. No one else would have helped – I thought I was done for.'

''S okay,' he muttered. He hadn't *planned* to help her; it had just been instinct – and it had nearly got him killed. But for some reason he'd felt like throwing all caution to the wind. Perhaps it was because of Marta; perhaps it was the sense of injustice.

He glanced down at Thea's arm, tucked tight against her stomach, and winced. He could see it was at an awkward angle.

'Doesn't it hurt?' he asked.

Thea rolled her eyes. 'What do you think?' Her gaze darted around. 'They've been standing watch over the dungeon for two days. I couldn't do a thing about it.'

'What could you have done anyway?' Quinn asked.

'Is anyone watching?' Thea whispered.

Quinn blinked stupidly. 'Huh?'

'Is anyone watching?' she repeated.

Quinn took a quick look around. All the recruits were tucking into their food as though it might be snatched away at any minute. On their own tables, the guards were piling plates high and slurping away at cups of wine.

'No.'

Thea winked at him. 'Then watch this.' She raised her good hand and began to chant under her breath. Her fingers danced as though she was playing a harp. Quinn felt the familiar tug of magic in the air, just as he had when his aunt had done her spells. This time it felt sharper, more powerful.

Beneath her sleeve, Thea's broken arm seemed to shift and straighten. Quinn bit his lip and his brow crunched with concentration. Whatever Thea was doing looked seriously painful, but she didn't even flinch as the bones moved in her arm. A moment later, she lifted her broken arm and wiggled her fingers. Quinn's jaw nearly hit the floor.

'Ah,' Thea sighed. 'That's better.'

'How did you . . . ?' he started.

'Shh . . . ' Thea hissed. 'Come closer.'

Checking around her one more time, Thea leaned over and touched the cut on Quinn's head – it had not yet healed since Jori had whacked him with the chain. He felt a sensation like a spider crawling on his forehead. His skin tugged uncomfortably as though something was pulling the two sides of the cuts, joining them and knitting them together. Then suddenly the cut was gone, healed. It was as if it had never been there.

Thea slumped forward, her face going pale, and Quinn caught her by the shoulder before she hit the table.

'That was incredible!' he hissed.

Slowly she pushed herself back up, shaking. The magic had completely drained her.

'Healing's harder than it looks, you know.'

'It looked *pretty* hard,' Quinn said.

She flashed him a weak smile. 'Well, it's the least I can do.'

The guards were shouting back and forth across the hall as they guzzled more and more wine. The older trainees were clustered together on other tables, muttering among themselves. No one was paying any attention to Quinn and Thea.

'How did you end up in here?' Quinn asked quietly. 'You don't seem like the usual poor kid from Yaross Island.'

Thea raised an eyebrow. 'Really? What do I seem like?'

Quinn coloured. 'I don't mean anything bad. I mean –' he swept a hand around to include the new trainees – 'look at us.' The recruits were all as scrawny as Quinn. Under her bruises, Thea looked healthy and well fed. 'And besides, I bet no one in here has magic skills like yours.'

'Well, I'm not from Yaross. I'm from the Rock of Sighs.'

'The one right in the middle of the sea?' Quinn asked.

'Yes,' Thea continued. 'It's so tiny that it isn't classed alongside the main Twelve Islands of Alariss. It's basically just a big rock with a small patch of land on it.'

Quinn looked confused. He thought being isolated in Rivervale was bad enough. 'Then why live there?'

'It's not like I had a choice!' Thea explained. 'My mother died when I was young and I've never known my father. I've lived there ever since I can remember, with my tutor, Telemus. Marshall Stant is the master of the island, even though he's only there once every year or two. When he visited this time, he found out that Telemus had been teaching me magic.'

'And he didn't like that?' Quinn asked.

'You can say that again,' Thea said. 'He brought me here to punish me. I don't know what happened to Telemus, but it can't have been good.'

Quinn felt for Thea – it was just like what Goric had done to him and Marta. The Black Guard didn't care about who they hurt as long as people followed their stupid rules. Suddenly, in amongst the bustling recruits who'd all ignored him, Quinn didn't feel quite so alone.

Quinn told Thea about his own life, and the endless persecution at Goric's hands.

'He burned down our cottage,' Quinn said. 'He didn't have to. He just wanted an excuse.' He felt the fury building up in him again and his skin grew hot as he remembered Goric throwing Marta to the ground. 'I thought the Black Guard were something to look up to,' he whispered. 'Now I know they're just keeping us down.'

Thea nodded grimly. 'The older people remember what it was like before the Black

Guard came.' She lowered her voice. 'When the Dragon Knights were here.'

Quinn's eyes darted across the hall. 'Shh. That kind of talk will get us killed!'

'*Any* kind of talk can get you killed round here,' Thea replied. 'That's the point. The Black Guard are evil and they have to be stopped.'

Quinn sat deep in thought. The Black Guard might be evil but who would stop them? The Dragon Knights were long gone. There was no one to protect them now.

After dinner, the recruits pushed the benches to the wall and set up their beds by the side of the tables, as usual. Except this time Quinn and Thea set up camp together, away from the other recruits. As the light fell, the guards extinguished the main fire and barked at the trainees to go to sleep. Even though Quinn was exhausted, his mind kept going over and over the events of the last few days. No matter what, he couldn't let himself become one of the Black Guard. They represented everything that was wrong with the

Islands. Somehow, he had to escape. He wondered if Thea could help, or if she'd even want to.

Quinn desperately needed sleep. He rearranged his bundle of clothes and blankets. All around him, the trainees and the new recruits were settled down by the tables of the Great Hall. Quinn covered his ears against the snoring and eventually drifted off into a deep doze.

However, disturbed by his own dreams, he woke abruptly in the dark.

Still half asleep, he propped himself up on his elbows and rubbed his eyes. The Great Hall was eerie in the darkness, with just the odd flaming torch flickering around the walls, casting shifting shadows across the floor and tables. From where he lay next to Thea, it looked to Quinn like giants made of shadows were stalking around the Great Hall.

He rolled over and tried to go back to sleep, but as he did so he gave a yelp . . .

'What the —' Something was digging in his side.

Marta's package!

He'd been so busy getting used to the garrison that he'd completely forgotten about it. Quinn rolled over and pulled out the heavy parcel that Marta had magically transported into his jacket. It had lain in a small knapsack the guards had given him for his meagre possessions over the last two days. Finally, he had a chance to see what it was.

Loud snores echoed around the hall as the other recruits dozed. Quinn peered out into the darkness but could barely see in front of his face. He decided to make for the flaming torch flickering in the alcove – that way he could get a proper look.

He pulled back his flimsy blanket and crawled across the sleeping bodies of several recruits. The parcel weighed heavily in his hands as he made his way through the murky half-light.

He scrambled across to the torch and was instantly bathed in its orange glow.

If a guard comes in now I'm dead meat, he thought. *Better make this quick.*

By the quivering torchlight, he slowly undid

the string. The package was long and thin and heavier than it looked. Whatever was inside was wrapped in several layers of cloth. He peeled the layers off one by one and held the package to the light. The golden blade of his father's emerald-handled dagger glinted back at him.

Quinn's heart leapt. *I thought it was lost!*

He swallowed, trying to hold back a gasp. The dagger was the only thing he had to remember his father, and now it was the only thing he had to remember Marta, too.

As he wrapped up the dagger once more he heard a shuffling noise behind him. He whirled around and peered into the darkness.

Nothing.

I must be imagining things, he thought, as he turned back to the dagger, lost in the memory of Goric's attack on his cottage.

But as he did so he felt a hand creep across his face and clamp down on his mouth. Then something fell over his head, and everything went black.

CHAPTER 8

THE HIGH TOWER

Quinn gasped and flailed at the coarse material that had been tossed over his head. Someone thumped into him and bundled him to the floor.

'Shh!' a voice hissed.

He twisted round and just made out a mess of red hair under the blanket. *Thea!*

'Don't move a muscle!' she whispered.

Footsteps sounded, crossing the flagstone floor towards them.

'Get over here!' a harsh voice barked.

Quinn's heart froze. *We've been spotted*, he thought.

Carefully, he lifted up the edge of the blanket and peered out. Goric was stomping across the hall, carrying his armour himself, trailed by a skinny page boy who couldn't have been more than seven or eight years old.

The pounding of his pulse in his ears quietened as Quinn realised Goric hadn't been shouting at *them*.

Goric was dressed in a sweat-stained brown shift and leggings. Although he was still twice Quinn's size, without the magical armour, Quinn could see he was just a man: a big, dangerous, violent, cruel man, but a man all the same. Quinn needed to remember that.

Goric turned slowly, his gaze drifting across the Great Hall; Quinn froze and dropped the blanket. They were in the shadows, but he was sure Goric was looking right at them. Quinn's heart was pounding so hard he was convinced Thea would be able to hear it. He held his breath. *Don't see us. Don't see us!*

The Captain of the Guard threw down his armour and sword with a clatter that made several of the recruits moan in their sleep – Quinn peaked out from under the blanket once more.

'Clean it!' Goric barked at the page. 'I want every inch of it shining like a mirror by the morning.'

The page stared up at him with frightened eyes. 'Th-there isn't time,' he stammered. The page's voice sounded like it was going to break.

Goric bared his teeth. They looked yellow and rotten in the torchlight.

'You'll do it,' he snarled, 'or tomorrow night it'll be some other page cleaning *your* blood off my sword. Got it?'

The page shrank back, nodding so hard it looked like his head might fly off. With a kick that sent the page to the flagstones, Goric turned away and strode back out of the hall. The page gathered up the armour, and staggering under its weight, headed out the other end of the hall towards the armoury.

When they were gone and the hall had settled back into snores, Quinn let out a groan of relief.

If it hadn't been for the blanket, he would be dead.

'Thanks,' he whispered, pulling off the blanket. 'That was close . . . '

Thea grinned. 'You saved me, and now I've saved you. Fair's fair, right?'

Quinn nodded in relief.

'Anyway,' she continued. 'What were you doing out of bed?'

'Nothing,' he shrugged. 'What are *you* doing out of bed?'

'My necklace,' Thea whispered. 'It used to belong to my mother. I wasn't planning on letting the guards keep it forever. I intend to get it back.'

The air in the Great Hall still smelled of woodsmoke and cooked meat, but now that the fire was out the air had turned cool.

Quinn shivered. 'Is that a good idea? If they catch you . . . '

'Of course it's a good idea,' Thea said. 'It's my idea. I'm not letting them keep it. Anyway, if we're going to survive this, we need to know what we're dealing with. We need to know this place as well as they do . . . unless you want to become one of them?'

'Gods, no!'

'Then come on. While everyone's asleep.'

Quinn followed Thea as she stepped carefully through the mass of sleeping bodies to a door on the far side of the hall. He knew the dangers, but couldn't help feeling excited as well; finally, he'd found someone who felt the same way as him about the Guard.

'I saw some guards go through here after the feast,' she whispered. 'I reckon it must be where they have their quarters.'

They slipped through the door into a dark corridor. Only a single torch was burning in a corner near the far end, where the corridor turned abruptly to the right. The doorways on either side were sunk in shadows. Quinn gritted his teeth. If someone came out of one of those doors now, they'd have no chance. But Thea was already striding boldly down the passageway. He hurried after her, stepping as quietly as he could.

They'd almost reached the end when a sudden, scratching noise made Quinn jump.

'What was that?' Thea hissed.

Footsteps echoed along the corridor, just around the corner.

'Someone's coming!' he murmured.

'Through here, quick!' Thea said. She pushed open a small door and Quinn didn't wait to see if anyone was on the other side before darting in after her.

They listened as the footsteps disappeared down the corridor.

Quinn breathed a sigh of relief. 'That was too close.'

'But exciting!' Thea laughed.

Quinn grinned – it was good to have someone fearless on his side.

'Yes, but now what?' he asked.

'Just watch!'

Suddenly, a tiny spark crackled into life right between Thea's hands. As it rose in the air, Quinn saw they were in a passage, which was now illuminated to reveal a spiral staircase.

Quinn smiled. 'You might come in handy round here.'

'I do try!' Thea chuckled. 'Come on, let's see what they're hiding up there.'

They crept up in the dark. Wooden steps creaked under Quinn's feet, but thankfully no sound came from below them.

As they reached the top, the staircase opened out into a dilapidated tower room. Dust lay thick on the floor and broken furniture had been piled against one wall. Boxes upon boxes filled the space on the floor. Faint moonlight filtered in through a couple of high, dirty windows. Quinn stepped up and took it all in. As he looked up at the wall something caught his eye: six enormous shields hanging from the walls around the room.

As he looked closer he gave a gasp of surprise. The Black Guard had shields, boring, metal shields. But *these* shields were clearly special. Each one was a different colour, faded now, but impressive for their huge size and ornate decorations. And each one depicted a fierce, fighting dragon.

'Where did *those* come from?' Thea gasped.

Quinn approached the nearest shield. On it, a red dragon curled around a banner on a long pole. The banner didn't show the black, clenched fist of the Empire. Instead, it showed a blazing sun.

'That's the flag of the old Emperor,' Thea whispered, impressed.

Quinn had seen this dragon before. It was the fiery-red dragon he'd spotted in Aunt Marta's spell. The next shield showed the blue-scaled wind dragon that had sent freezing air over the attacking Black Guard.

'The Dragon Knights,' Quinn breathed. 'They must have carried these in their human form!'

In the sunlight, when they were new, the shields must have been magnificent, but Emperor Vayn's Black Guard had used them for target practice till they were scraped and worn, arrows jutting out of them at every angle. Still, the detail painted on them was incredible. Every scale on each dragon's skin was picked out in tiny brush strokes.

'Look at this,' Thea said. She pulled an iron box out from beneath a dusty old chair. Quinn peered over her shoulder as she opened it. In the shadows, Quinn made out jewellery and coins stashed inside the box.

Thea tugged out a thin golden chain with a pendant on the end. 'My necklace!'

'And look at all this other stuff,' Quinn said. 'The guards must have been stealing from the trainees for years.'

Thea stepped forward and tugged one of the arrows from the flame dragon's shield. She threw it onto the ground, shaking her head. Quinn remembered what Marta had showed him in the fire vision and what she'd told him about the Dragon Knights.

'Do you think the Dragon Knights were as evil as everyone says?' he asked.

'As evil as the Black Guard and Emperor Vayn tell us, you mean? Of course not!' Thea scoffed. 'They weren't evil at all.' She stared up at the shield above her. 'That was Ignus, the Flame Dragon. Do you know, when pirates raided the villages on the shores of Aya Sur, he flew all the way from the Imperial Castle and drove them away? Can you imagine the Black Guard bothering?'

She moved on to the next. 'And this was Kyria the Water Dragon. She used to fly out in storms to help the fishing fleets get home safely.'

Thea moved around the room, naming Nord the Storm Dragon, Ulric the Shadow Dragon, Noctaris the Night Dragon and Taric the Mirror Dragon. 'They were all brave, and they kept the kingdom safe, until Vayn betrayed it.'

Quinn listened hard.

'And that's not all,' Thea continued. 'Apparently the surviving Dragon Knights are still out there, somewhere, roaming the Twelve Islands in their human form.'

'How do you know all that?' Quinn gasped. 'Surely that's forbidden knowledge.'

Thea shrugged. 'My mother was a Lady of the Imperial Court.' Her mouth tugged down, and she turned away quickly so Quinn couldn't see her face. 'All I know is that she died shortly after the old Emperor Marek. When I was left in Telemus's care, he told me the old stories about the dragons. I don't know if it's all true, but the dragons can't have been worse than the Black Guard, can they?'

Quinn shook his head. 'My aunt didn't think so . . . What about your father?'

Thea looked down. 'I have no idea. Telemus never spoke of him. I think he was killed when Vayn took the Imperial Castle. Lots of people were.' She cleared her throat again.

Quinn suddenly felt awkward. He knew what it felt like when he had to talk about how his parents had died when he was a baby. It had always made him want to shrink inside his own clothes until he'd completely disappeared. But at least he had a friend in Thea, someone who knew how it felt.

He turned away and sat cross-legged on the floor to unwrap his package – ready to show Thea.

'Look,' Quinn said. The emerald-handled dagger lay on the cloth. Carefully, Quinn took hold of the handle and pulled the dagger from its leather sheath; the blade glinted in the dim light.

'It's beautiful,' Thea said.

'This is all I have left of my parents,' he replied. 'It's my father's dagger. I know how you feel.'

Thea reached out to touch it but suddenly the dagger jerked back, as if moving away from her.

'Huh?' Quinn jumped up and held on to it as the blade squirmed in his hand.

'What's happening?' Thea gasped.

Bit by bit, the dagger seemed to grow longer. Its blade lengthened and widened. The handle swelled in Quinn's hand. Within seconds, Quinn was holding a mighty golden sword. Its blade was as long as Quinn's arm and flashed in the dim light.

'Magic!' Thea gasped.

As Quinn looked closer he noticed the fine writing etched across its length. He recognised it as the ancient dragon language, although he couldn't read it. The handle had changed from the plain, smooth emerald to a dragon's head, its mouth open in a snarl, teeth and tongue ready to strike.

Golden light sparkled suddenly in the cloth wrappings and a piece of folded paper appeared where the dagger had lain a moment ago. Carefully, Quinn unfolded it. It was written in Marta's neat, precise handwriting.

'"This is your father's sword,"' Quinn read. '"It will guide and protect you. Keep it safe, and do not let the Black Guard see it."'

'Wow,' Thea said. She sounded impressed. 'Your father must have been important.'

Quinn shook his head. 'My father was a fisherman. I have no idea why he'd have something like this.'

'Try it out,' Thea said, eagerly.

He swung the sword around his head and it sliced easily through the air. It hardly felt like he was swinging a sword at all and the handle fitted perfectly in his palm.

He brought the sword down then peered at

the blade, looking closer at the fine writing etched into it.

Quinn's reflection seemed to swirl in the bright metal of the sword and then, just for a second, he saw something.

With a yell, he dropped the sword. It clattered to the floor and he jumped back. Released from his hands, the sword had shrunk back to a simple dagger again.

'What is it?' Thea demanded. 'What happened?'

Quinn shook his head. 'Nothing. It was nothing. I just . . . '

But Quinn didn't finish his sentence. When he'd looked into the sword, he hadn't seen his own face looking back at him. He'd seen a golden dragon.

And it had been watching him with eyes that were as real as his own.

CHAPTER 9

TRAINING DAY

Quinn woke to the sound of metal crashing on metal.

He groaned and rolled over. His head was thumping already. At the far end of the Great Hall, one of the guards was hammering his sword against a large pan.

'Get up, you lazy scum!' he bellowed. 'Move yourselves!'

Quinn had barely slept. His mind had been whirring away trying to figure everything out. Thea agreed that the dragons weren't evil, but there had been one watching him from the sword. Quinn wanted to know why.

He also couldn't understand why his father would have a sword like that in the first place. Quinn knew only a lord or a marshall like Stant would have something like that. But his father hadn't been anyone important.

A hand grabbed Quinn and hauled him out from under the table. His head bounced off the bottom of the bench as he was dragged past.

'What do you think this is . . . ?' Jarin shouted into his ear.

'. . . A holiday?' Rowena finished.

She kicked Quinn up the backside. He jumped forward before she could swing for him again. All along the hall, new recruits were being shoved and kicked towards the entrance. As he hurriedly hid the knapsack with his father's dagger in his bundle of sheets, shoving it into his corner of the hall, he saw Thea scramble out from under the bench and saw her shoved into a separate group. Today he was on his own.

Out in the courtyard, the recruits were pushed

into a ragged line. Goric stalked up in front of them. Quinn stood as still as he could, staring straight ahead, determined not to catch the Captain's eye.

'Look at you!' Goric sneered at the trainees. 'You're pathetic weaklings, all of you. Not a single one of you deserves to be in the Black Guard. And you stink!' He wrinkled his nose. 'At least we can do something about that.'

Before the trainees could react, several of the guards came up behind them with buckets of icy water – the morning ritual. Quinn let out a cry as freezing water smashed into him. His hair dripped onto his face and his shirt stuck to his skin. He thanked the heavens he'd left his package hidden in his knapsack – if he'd kept it with him it would have shown through his soaking clothes.

Another guard dropped a pile of black tunics in the dirt.

'You've been here long enough,' Goric roared. 'Now you owe your loyalty and your life to the Emperor Vayn, you should dress like a Black Guardsman.'

A couple of days is all it takes to forget Marta? To become loyal to the Black Guard? Quinn wondered. *I don't think so.*

Shivering, he tugged off his soaked shirt and pulled on a plain black tunic and trousers. Around him, the other trainees dressed. Seeing them clothed in black made Quinn feel even colder than the water had. Goric would turn all of these shivering recruits into guards just like him and then let them loose to terrorise the Islands. If the dragon in the sword was trying to contact him, he knew there was a chance to stop the Guard before that happened.

'You!' Goric spat, stopping in front of Quinn.

What have I done now? he wondered.

'We all saw you fight Jori,' Goric said loudly. Laughs came from the guards and some mean hisses from the older recruits. 'A great warrior like you obviously doesn't need to train like the other recruits.'

'I —' Quinn started, but Goric didn't let him speak.

'This scrawny nobody,' Goric said, as he stood

before the older trainees, 'thinks he's a great hero. Who agrees?'

The trainees curled their lips and jeered. Quinn felt himself rage under their hate-filled eyes.

'And who thinks he is a pathetic, ungrateful, disloyal little worm?'

The trainees muttered agreement.

'Today,' Goric said, 'we will be learning basic sword craft.' He strode over to Quinn. 'Imagine this is – I don't know – let's say some foolish washer boy who betrayed his loyalty to the Emperor.'

Quinn fumed. Goric was clearly determined to make his life hell.

'We'd have to teach him a lesson, wouldn't we?' Goric drew his weapon and threw a flimsy wooden sword towards Quinn. It felt clumsy and badly balanced.

'Now watch!' Goric shouted, as he stabbed the point of his sword towards Quinn. Quinn tried to parry, but the wooden sword felt heavy and awkward compared with his father's golden sword.

'Twist!' Goric shouted as he thrust the sword. With a shudder, Quinn dashed out of the way, before the sword could rip through his guts. He twisted his own battered sword.

'Overhand, trainees,' Goric said, and this time he swung his sword up and over, bringing it down like a hammer onto Quinn's weak sword. Quinn couldn't help but flinch as the wooden sword shattered in two.

Goric just laughed and sneered at Quinn. 'Not so clever now, are we?'

Anger bubbled up inside Quinn. *How was that a fair fight?* he raged. *If I'd had my father's sword . . .*

Goric strode back to the trainees. 'In the old days, we faced the most evil of foes: dragons! Beasts so fierce they could fry you with a single breath, with talons so long and so sharp they could rip you open like a ripe plum. After three years at Yaross Garrison, you will know how to fight them.'

Three years, Quinn repeated to himself. He wasn't planning on staying more than three days.

'The dragons were inhuman and evil. They terrorised the land that they were supposed to protect and they killed the Imperial Family. The Emperor Vayn gave people the power to fight back.' The Captain crashed his gauntlet against his armour. 'The black armour. No weapon can pierce it.'

Goric gestured to the guard, Jarin, who was waiting nearby. He ran over, carrying a bow and a quiver of arrows. Goric pulled out an arrow and placed it on the bowstring, then drew it back and spun towards Quinn. The arrow shot past, almost clipping his ear. It flew through the courtyard gate and thumped into a target in a field far beyond. Quinn had never seen an arrow fired so far, but he was about to see something even stranger.

Goric raised his hand. The arrow quivered in the target, then came loose. It shot back through the gate and across the courtyard. Quinn had to duck as it rushed past again and slapped back into Goric's hand.

Magic! Of course. Goric was strutting around,

showing off the magical weapons Emperor Vayn had given them.

'Arrows that always return to the man who shot them, so you never run out,' Goric boasted.

Jarin handed Goric a sword in a scabbard. When Goric drew it out, it blazed with ice despite the hot sunshine that was now beating down. Rowena staggered over carrying the carcass of a wild boar. Goric stabbed the carcass with the blazing sword. Ice rushed over the boar's body, and when Goric pulled out the sword, the carcass shattered into a million frozen pieces. He lifted the sword again.

'These are the weapons the Emperor Vayn gave to us to defend ourselves from the evil Dragon Knights . . . and those who side with the Dragon Knights against the people of this land.'

He spun around, sweeping the sword up and round, right towards Quinn. Ice glittered in the sunlight. The blade stopped so close to his face he could feel the frost.

'One touch of the blade will freeze a man solid,' Goric growled.

Quinn flinched back, away from the icy blade. Goric leaned over him, eyes filled with hate and Quinn knew then there was nothing he could do to stop Goric despising him. The Captain of the Guard would be his enemy for life. If the Dragon Knights were still out there, he had to get out and find them. It was his only hope.

That evening, Quinn stumbled into the Great Hall half an hour later than the other recruits. Goric had made him stay behind to clear the courtyard, and when he was finally finished his stomach was so empty it hurt. All the food would be gone, and he knew Goric had done it on purpose. He swore to himself that he wouldn't let Goric break him.

Thea was waiting for him at the table as everyone was getting ready to bed down for the night. As he slipped in, sure he was going to spend the night hungry, Thea lifted her blanket and showed him a plate piled high with food.

'They had me on kitchen duties after training,'

she explained. 'At least there's one advantage to cleaning pans . . . '

Quinn could have hugged her.

That was enough for him. He had to trust someone, and Thea was the only one who'd shown any concern for him. And she knew about dragons. Maybe she would know about the dragon in his sword, too.

'I need to talk to you,' he said, tucking into a cold mouthful of food. 'In the tower room, tonight.'

She gave him a curious look. 'What about?'

'I'll tell you there.' He glanced around the packed Great Hall. 'I might have found us a way out of here.'

Thea nodded. 'Then let's do it. Let's make this the last night in this place!'

CHAPTER 10

THE BEGINNINGS OF A PLAN

Quinn woke with a start just as the first glimmer of half-light began sneaking in through the high windows. He rolled over and prodded Thea's shoulder.

'Thea, we're late,' he whispered. 'Get up!'

Thea wearily rubbed her eyes and pushed her big red mane of hair away from her face. Quinn recognised the heavy sense of fatigue, but there was no time to be lazing around. The other recruits would be awake soon enough.

'Get up, now!' he hissed.

Thea grumbled and scrambled to her feet. 'This'd better be worth it.'

'You just wait!' Quinn replied.

Together, they sneaked through the Great Hall then hurried along the corridor towards the small door and the tower room. Snores filled the hall behind them, and trainees shifted and muttered in their sleep.

At last they reached the door near the end of the corridor and pulled it open. The spiral stairs reached up into the semi-darkness in front of them. Quinn smiled. He couldn't wait to get back to that tower room and see those incredible shields again. They'd be safe up there, away from the hell of their training and Goric's bullying. They'd be able to think of a plan out of the sight of the cruel guard.

Quinn bounded up the stairs with Thea right behind, but suddenly he came to an abrupt halt, clanging into a solid mass of black armour. He recognised the mean, scarred face in front of him and stared in horror.

Rowena!

With a startled grunt she grabbed him by the arm and practically lifted him off the ground.

'And just where do you think *you're* going?'

Quinn winced at the pain in his arm. He hadn't noticed Rowena come round the corner, but now she was right in his face and there was no place to turn.

'Get off me!' he cried.

'I don't think so, boy,' she sneered. 'Not until you tell me why you're out of bed.'

Quinn tried to wriggle out of her grip – Goric would have their heads on poles.

Quinn gave Thea a frantic look as he tried desperately to think of something, but Thea had her eyes closed, as if she was trying to block the whole thing out.

What's she doing? Quinn thought. *This is not the time for a nap!*

Rowena was becoming impatient and started marching Quinn back down the stairs, when suddenly he heard a soft chanting noise come from Thea. Gradually the noise became louder and soon the magic was pulsing out in waves.

'What's she —' Rowena began, but she didn't have a chance to finish. A weird purple mist pulsed out from Thea, as soft as a spider's web, covering her completely.

A spell!

Rowena's eyes rolled in her skull – she looked like a woman possessed. She peered down at Quinn and Thea as if they'd come from another land.

'W-what am I doing here?' she asked.

Quinn just muttered. 'Erm . . . you're passing through . . . '

'. . . To the kitchen,' Thea finished.

'That's right,' Rowena mumbled. Her terrifying scowl had gone and was replaced with a happy grin that looked completely the wrong shape for her face. 'Then I'll be on my way . . . '

She blinked, then let go of Quinn's arm and fumbled all the way down the stairs to the bottom and out of the door.

Quinn sagged in relief. 'What *was* that?'

Thea grinned smugly. 'Just a little amnesia spell. It used to come in pretty handy when I wanted to avoid my tutor.'

Quinn shook his head in wonder. 'Just so long as you don't use it on me!'

'I will unless you tell us what we're doing here!' Thea joked, and then she turned serious. 'The spell won't last forever, Quinn, so we'd better be quick.'

'OK, listen,' he said, as the two of them entered the tower room. 'You know about dragons, don't you?'

Thea shrugged. 'I know some stories.'

Which was more than Quinn knew. He'd never wanted to listen when Marta had talked about the Dragon Knights. Now he wished he had.

'Did you ever hear anything about a sword?' He frowned. 'Or maybe about a dragon that could contact you through metal?'

She gave him a curious look. 'The stories said that mirror dragons could look through any reflective surfaces. Shiny metal would work, I guess. Why?'

Quinn grinned. 'Because I saw one!'

Thea's eyes widened in astonishment. Quinn laughed at her expression.

'You do know you're crazy, right?' Thea said. 'The Dragon Knights were all bound. They can't use their powers any more, and every minor who shows any signs of dragonblood has to report to the Black Guard.'

The penalty for any dragonblood who didn't turn themselves in was instant death. No one would risk it. But Quinn knew what he'd seen. *There was a dragon in the sword, and it was looking right at me!*

'But there could be one,' Quinn said. 'Couldn't there? You said yourself that they were out there somewhere. Maybe if we can contact one of them they'll help us get out of here. We can do something about Vayn and the Black Guard and the unfairness of it all.' Quinn's chest tightened and flared hot.

'But Telemus told me dragonblood is dying out,' Thea said. 'No one has seen an actual dragon for years.'

Shaking his head, Quinn pulled out Marta's package. Carefully he unwrapped the emerald-handled knife. When he took it in his hand, it grew swiftly into the sword again, like it was made for only his hand. *Thank the gods for that!* He'd wondered if it had been a dream.

'Look at this.' He held it out in front of Thea.

She peered into the blade, and then shook her head. 'All I can see is my reflection.' She pushed back her long red hair and plucked at her scruffy black tunic. 'This *really* doesn't suit me.'

Quinn moved in next to her. Thea's reflection stared back at them as clear as day – Quinn saw her pale skin and green eyes – but where Quinn's face should have been, a golden dragon looked back. Two narrow horns swept back over the dragon's head; a ridge of sharp scales jutted out above the eyes, which were the same deep amber of Quinn's own. Long, sharp teeth glittered as the dragon's mouth opened. Quinn realised his own mouth was hanging open, and he closed it with a snap. The dragon did the same.

'See!' he said.

Thea looked up in astonishment. 'Quinn. That's no mirror dragon.'

'What are you talking about? Look!' Quinn practically shouted.

'No, you don't get it,' Thea continued. 'That's not a mirror dragon. That's *you*!'

Quinn stared at her. In the sword, the reflection of the dragon stared back at Thea.

'*What?*'

'You must have dragonblood,' Thea said. 'Quinn, I don't know what it is about that sword but it's clearly special. It's showing you your *dragonform.*'

Quinn had no idea what she was talking about. His dragonform? He didn't have a dragonform. *If I was a dragonblood, someone would have noticed. Wouldn't they?* It was crazy. Nuts. Maybe she'd banged her head too hard in training and now she was talking gibberish.

He shook his head. The dragon reflected in the sword shook its golden head too.

'How can I?' Quinn burst out. 'I'm from Yaross . . . '

'That doesn't matter – dragons are from all over the place.'

'But wouldn't someone have told me? Wouldn't Marta —'

'Wouldn't Marta what?' Thea asked.

'Marta would have told me,' Quinn continued, lowering the sword. 'Except, it turns out there was a lot she didn't tell me – like how she was in the Royal Court, too. Just like your mother.'

Thoughts came rushing in all at once. If he really were a dragonblood, he would be able to transform into a real dragon. He would have powers. In the court of the Emperor Marek, he could have been a Dragon Knight, flying across the skies and defending the Islands.

But the Emperor Marek was long dead, and dragons were outcasts now.

'Then maybe she didn't tell you about this,' Thea suggested.

'I can't be a dragon,' he whispered. 'Dragonbloods aren't allowed. I'll have to turn myself in to be bound. Or the penalty will be death.'

Thea glared fiercely at him. 'What are you talking about? You're just repeating what the

к Guard tell people. There's nothing shameful
ɔout being a dragonblood. The Dragon Knights
were heroes. You should hear some of the things
Noctaris the Night Dragon and Ignus the Flame
Dragon did. They were great men!'

As Thea said each of the names, there was a
flash inside the sword. Quinn squinted at the metal.

'Say the names again.'

'Ignus the Flame Dragon,' Thea said.

The sword in Quinn's hand tugged violently
to the left. Quinn let it move. It swung to point
at the wall. Inside the blade an image formed
of a huge man hunched over a blacksmith's
forge, hammering at a breastplate. Sparks flew
from his great hammer.

'I don't get it,' Quinn said. 'What's happening?'

'It's like a compass,' Thea said excitedly. 'I
think it's pointing to where the Dragon Knights
have hidden themselves. Don't you get it?
Somehow, your sword can lead us to the Dragon
Knights. To your kin!'

Quinn frowned. 'Yes, but . . . '

'Yes, but nothing! If you don't want to spend

the rest of your life bound and shunned by everyone, you need to find the Dragon Knights. They'll know what to do.'

Quinn didn't want to be bound, but he didn't know if he wanted dragonblood either. No one would ever talk to him. They might not even let him back in the village. But then, if it put him on the opposite side to the Black Guard . . .

'You're right. I can't stay here,' he said. The Black Guard would find out about his dragonblood. They always did. And Goric would take great pleasure in executing him.

'Good!' Thea said. 'And I'm not staying either. I never wanted to be in the Black Guard anyway.'

She grinned suddenly. 'Come on! It's time we got out of here!'

CHAPTER II

A BID FOR FREEDOM

Thea and Quinn ran from the tower room and straight into trouble.

Rowena was standing at the bottom of the stairs, looking confused, as though she couldn't remember why she was there. Quinn managed to catch himself before he knocked her clean over. He dropped his head, so he wouldn't catch her eye. Maybe if she was confused enough, she wouldn't notice them.

But Quinn had forgotten he was still carrying his father's sword. Rowena could hardly miss seeing that.

The guard's eyes widened and she glowered at them. The purple mist was fading and she was suddenly much more alert. 'Wait a minute . . . ' she gasped, 'I know you . . . '

'Uh-oh. I think that spell might have worn off,' Thea hissed.

Quinn gulped. 'We . . . ah . . . we're running an errand for Goric,' he lied.

Rowena narrowed her eyes and reached out for Quinn with a great, gauntleted hand. 'Let's see about that, shall we?'

Rowena lunged and Quinn skipped out of the way.

If she takes us to Goric, the game will be up before we've even had a chance!

The guard turned to follow, fury lining her face. Quinn had to do something. He swiped at Rowena's legs with the flat of the blade of his father's sword. With a yelp, she was knocked off her feet. As she struggled for balance on the slippery stone steps, Quinn leapt forward and brought the hilt of his sword down over her head. She collapsed, out cold.

'Uh-oh,' Thea gasped. 'We've really done it now. Once she comes round she's going to alert the whole garrison.'

'Then we'd better not stick around,' Quinn yelled. 'Go!'

Quinn and Thea raced down the final few steps and out into the corridor. The morning light was streaming through the high windows now and Quinn could hear the trainees being rudely awoken by the guards in the hall.

Quinn cursed. He'd hoped they'd be out before anyone was awake, but he should have known Goric would be up with the sun. Quinn and Thea had no choice but to mingle with the rest of them. He made a makeshift sheath for his sword with his jacket, and lazily hung his black shirt over the waistband of his trousers, hoping to disguise the hilt.

'What are we going to do?' Thea hissed.

'Try to keep our heads down,' Quinn said. 'If we can get to the gateway, maybe we can sneak out without anyone noticing.'

Some hope, he thought bitterly. *But what else can we do?*

They followed the first of the yawning trainees out to the courtyard. The recruits barely gave Quinn and Thea a second glance. For once Quinn was more than happy to be ignored.

'Look,' Quinn said, pointing to mops and a bucket resting beside the door. 'Pretend we're on cleaning duties, then maybe no one will bother us.'

They snatched up the mops and made their way across the courtyard, trying to look as though they had something important to do. On the other side of the open space, Goric was inspecting the Guard, peering closely at their armour and weapons. Quinn kept his eye on Goric as he and Thea strolled casually across.

Whilst Goric was busy shouting at a terrified recruit, Quinn pulled Thea into the shadow of the huge wall that surrounded the garrison.

'Look!' Quinn hissed. 'The portcullis is open for morning deliveries. This is our chance!'

Hurrying, they turned towards the gateway

and the raised portcullis. Guards stood on either side of the gate. Quinn's shoulders were stiff with tension, and he felt a trickle of sweat running down his back. He clenched his teeth but kept moving.

Suddenly a voice barked out from behind them. 'Stop them!'

Quinn spun around to see Rowena stumble out of the garrison building, clasping her head in one hand. She jabbed her finger at Quinn and Thea with the other. 'Stop!' she shouted again, drawing her sword. 'They're trying to escape!'

On the far side of the courtyard, Captain Goric caught sight of Quinn and Thea.

'Grab them!' he roared. 'Bring them to me!'

'Uh-oh,' Thea murmured. 'Let's get out of here . . . !'

The line of guards broke into a run. By the gate, a guardsman began untying the rope that held up the portcullis. Quinn stared around. It was hopeless. They were still too far away from the gateway. They'd never reach it before the guards caught them, and there was nowhere else they could run to. They were trapped!

'What are we going to do?' Quinn shouted.

Thea raised her hands, chanting a spell. Quinn pulled out his sword from the makeshift sheath. He knew even Thea's magic wasn't strong enough to defeat the whole of the Black Guard. He was going to have to fight.

Quinn turned to see the straw dragon at the far end of the courtyard. Just yesterday, the trainees had been using the dragon as target practice. But now, the dragon was beginning to glow. Fire sprang up into its eyes, as though it was coming to life. Then the whole straw dragon exploded into flame, sending heat searing across the courtyard. Guards dived for the ground as Thea worked her magic.

'Keep going!' cried Quinn.

He grabbed Thea's arm and together they dashed for the exit.

One of the guards at the gate unsheathed his long sword and raced towards them. The second guard finished untethering the rope and followed.

The portcullis began to ratchet slowly down, the metal spikes heading for the ground, cutting them off.

Quinn slashed at the first guard's legs. His golden sword was light and easy; it was like it wasn't even there. The blade carved its way into the guard's armoured shin plates and took his legs from under him, flinging him into the air. He crashed on the ground with a crunching thud of metal and bone. With a backswing right into the second guard's chest, Quinn sent him tumbling backwards, helplessly grappling the air for support.

Quinn dodged around the fallen men and ran full tilt for the gateway. Behind them, the rest of the Black Guard were chasing after them.

'Go!' Quinn yelled, shoving Thea towards the gateway.

Thea ducked down and scrambled under the iron grille. She turned to watch as the portcullis's spiky prongs plunged towards the ground.

Quinn was still on the wrong side.

CHAPTER 12

GOLDEN SCALES

Quinn leapt for the rope holding the portcullis. He slashed his sword as high as he could. It cut through the rope as easily as it would through a spider's web. The end of the rope whipped up.

'Catch us now, guard,' Quinn hissed and dived forwards.

Desperately, he rolled under the grille, metal spikes plunging towards him. Thea grabbed his arm and pulled. His feet shot through just as the portcullis crashed down behind him. He felt the dry ground shudder beneath him as the spikes drove into the dirt.

Thea pulled him up as the guards sprinted towards the gateway. Quinn didn't know how long the portcullis would hold.

'Come on!' Thea cried, tugging at him.

'Get back here,' Goric spat. 'No one leaves the Guard and gets away with it.'

'We'll make you pay!' Rowena hissed, as she pressed her face to the metal bars.

'We'll see!' Quinn taunted her, as he turned and ran.

Quinn knew the Black Guard wouldn't like being beaten by two trainees. They would be furious and humiliated. They would do anything to bring him and Thea back and make an example of them. They'd have to move fast.

Together they raced down the dirt road, checking over their shoulders as they went.

They had hardly gone half a mile, pumping their legs with all the strength they had, before Quinn heard the sound of screeching metal followed by hooves clattering on the road.

'They've opened the portcullis,' he said, panting for breath. 'They're coming!'

It was too soon! Quinn had thought they might be able to get back to the village before the Guard got free; maybe they could lie low. There was no way he and Thea would get to safety, now.

'Look, there!' Thea cried. She grabbed Quinn's arm and dragged him off the road, into a small, overgrown clearing. 'We have to hide . . . '

Quinn and Thea hacked their way through the prickly bushes and landed straight in a muddy ditch. Huge ropes of ivy dangled like a screen above them, and thick-trunked trees pressed in from all sides.

Quinn pressed his face to the dirt. All sorts of insects crawled over him and the stench was almost overpowering. The summer sun was already harsh and the heat bore down like an iron fist.

In the distance they could feel the horses thundering down the road and hear the guards hollering. Soon they came dangerously close, but the horses didn't slow down and Quinn let out a relieved breath as he saw their dark, sweating flanks streaking past.

'We did it,' Quinn muttered.

'See you later, Yaross Garrison!' Thea smiled, breathlessly.

Once Quinn and Thea had clambered out of the ditch, damp and covered in dirt, the pair made their way up and out towards the giant oak forest. The sun was high in the sky and it was well past midday when they finally found a thin trail that snaked its way through the trees. Climbing up the steep slope, they grabbed on to the gnarled exposed roots to help them. It was slow going, especially with the lush foliage encroaching on all sides. Quinn and Thea had to stop to hack away vines and bat away giant venomous insects. The dense forest was full of the calls of strange creatures, shrieks and yells of mysterious animals that scurried away in the undergrowth whenever they approached.

Suddenly Quinn realised why Marta had always told him to stay away from this place. There was an eerie feeling in the dim forest surroundings. He and Thea steered away from the huge red plants, which turned their flowery heads slowly as they passed, as if ready to strike out, and they both tried to ignore the feeling that they were being watched from the trees.

At last, they hauled themselves up onto a ridge and out into open terrain, where the trees were sparser. From this height Quinn could see the garrison building in the distance and Black Guard messengers darting back and forth. To the east the Floating Mountains sat in the sky, casting an ethereal shadow over the land.

'Let's rest for a second,' he called to Thea, as he slumped down on the ground.

'At last,' she panted.

For a moment Quinn could relax and breathe normally. The relief of being away from the Yaross Garrison was overwhelming. He'd told himself he wasn't going to spend three years there and he was right. He breathed in the heady freedom and let the sunlight wash over him. It no longer felt oppressive and hot.

Then, to the west, he gazed out and spotted his village, Rivervale, nestled in the crook of the

River Yar. Near the far edge, just a tiny speck on the landscape, were the blackened remains of his aunt's cottage. They'd never had much before, but now they had nothing. His calm evaporated, and he felt the familiar tight fury begin to build inside him once more.

This is Goric's fault, Quinn thought, *all of it . . .*

As the rage slowly built, a sudden pain flared across his chest. It felt like a million hot needles were dancing all over his skin and burning right through it. Quinn lifted up his tunic and gasped. The skin over his chest had turned to golden scales. His dragonblood was starting to manifest itself.

'Look!' he whispered, as the pain ebbed away.

Thea's eyes widened with surprise. 'You're coming into your dragonform . . . '

I really am turning into a dragon! he thought, as he ran his finger over the scales. They felt as smooth as stones in a river and they were hot and strong and strangely beautiful.

'But how?' Quinn asked.

'Well,' Thea began, 'according to Telemus, dragonblood manifests itself at around your age. They used to say it was triggered by uncontrollable emotion. Anger, hatred, love: anything extreme.'

That fits, Quinn thought. Whenever he thought of Marta and Goric the anger built inside him. That's what had happened when the guards had burned his house – he just hadn't realised it before.

'Then, as you grow older,' Thea continued, 'you eventually learn to control it . . . hopefully.'

Quinn looked down. His scales were starting to fade as his anger lessened, but he could still feel the strength in them.

'And then what?' he asked.

'Then you get to be a real dragon,' Thea said. 'Like a sand dragon or a stone dragon . . . Not just a skinny boy with a scaly chest . . . '

'Hey!' Quinn laughed, shoving Thea. 'You'd better watch out when I start breathing fire!'

As he looked out into the distance, Quinn let his mind wander. Being a stone dragon would be awesome. He would be able to drive the Black Guard right off Yaross Island so they never hurt anyone again. A fire dragon would be amazing too. Even a sand dragon, whatever that was. He wouldn't care what he was, as long as it meant he could fight the Black Guard.

He caught himself. Only a few days ago, he'd thought that dragons were evil. Everyone else in Alariss still did. Anyone who saw him and his scales would report him straight away. He'd have to find a way to change their minds.

'We should figure out where we're going,' Thea said, as they got ready to set off. 'We can't just keep running, and if we stay here too long, they'll find us. Use your sword.'

'Huh?' Quinn asked.

'Like in the tower room . . . It will lead us to the nearest Dragon Knight.'

Quinn drew his sword and peered at the reflection of his dragonform.

'Ignus,' he said, uttering the first of the dragon names he could think of. 'The Flame Dragon.'

Immediately, the sword turned to point east.

Quinn's reflection faded and was replaced by the image of the giant blacksmith labouring away in his forge. Then that image faded too and Quinn saw giant floating mountains high in the sky.

'That's on the other side of Yaross Island,' Quinn said, pointing. 'It isn't so far.'

'It's far enough,' Thea said, peering into the distance. 'If we have to walk, it could take days. How are we going to stay hidden that long?'

Quinn peered out across the landscape. Lush green forest gave way to rocky terrain; a dirt road carved its way through the open plain, where the farmers and labourers of Yaross Island scuttled around like ants.

'The road,' Quinn murmured. 'Follow me, I have an idea.'

Quinn darted across the open hilltop with Thea close behind. He headed east this time, back down the hill and into the forest once more.

The further they went, the stranger the forest became. Huge blue butterflies streamed through the trees like a fluttering river suspended in the sky. Strange multi-coloured insects followed them, as if expecting an easy meal.

At last, when neither of them could walk or run any further, they slumped down by the forest edge. Quinn reckoned they must have left at least a few miles between them and the garrison, but it was hard to tell when they were moving through the dense forest. From where they stood, the great road curved beneath them like a dusty river.

'We should keep out of sight,' Thea said. 'Just in case anyone's coming this way.'

'Someone coming our way is exactly what I'm hoping for . . . ' Quinn said.

'Huh?' Thea asked.

'Look, there!' Quinn pointed. On the road, a farmer was driving a spacious-looking wagon stacked with sacks. 'If we hurry we can catch him!'

They sprung out from the forest edge and down onto the main road just as the horse-drawn wagon came around the corner. They jumped and waved until the farmer brought the wagon to a stop.

'We're looking for a village with a forge and a blacksmith,' Quinn said, breathlessly. 'Do you know one?'

The farmer scratched his head, looking them up and down. 'Most villages have blacksmiths round here.'

'We know,' Quinn said. 'But this one's special. It's in the shadow of the Floating Mountains.'

The farmer scratched himself again. 'Hillshade,' he said, gruffly. 'That'll take you a few days' walk at least.'

Quinn noticed him look awry at their black tunics. They hadn't had anything to change into since leaving the garrison.

'We need to get there quickly,' Thea said, flashing him a smile. 'Do you think you could take us?' She pulled out a small silver coin from inside her tunic and held it up. 'We'd be really grateful.'

That seemed to do it. The farmer finally softened and grinned, showing several missing teeth. 'That's the kind of gratitude I could get used to.' He jerked his thumb towards the half-full wagon. 'Make yourselves comfortable – I'll have you there by morning.'

Feeling a great flood of relief wash over him, Quinn helped Thea to clamber in and they lay back in the wagon. With the sacks all around them, no one riding past would see them hiding. Once again Quinn could relax and put all thoughts of Yaross Garrison and the Black Guard's cruelty behind him. They were on the way to the Dragon Knights – and nothing could stop them now.

CHAPTER 13

THE BLACKSMITH'S FORGE

Quinn, Thea and the farmer travelled for the rest of the day. Quinn and Thea hid in the back of the wagon by daylight, but once it was dark they let themselves ride openly, feeling the cool night air on their skin. They passed the night in the wagon, the stars above them in the heavens.

By early morning they were on their way again and they soon came in sight of the Floating Mountains, hovering high above the ground, casting long shadows over the forest. Pink clouds wrapped around the craggy rocks like shawls. .

Thea looked at them curiously. 'I've never seen anything so beautiful. We heard about them back home, but I never expected to see them . . . '

For once, Quinn felt a sense of pride in Yaross.

'How do they stay up there?' asked Thea.

Quinn wondered how to explain it. They'd been like that forever, as long as history. There were all sorts of myths and legends: huge battles between magical gods or weird seismic events that had thrown the mountains into the air.

He vaulted off the wagon and ran alongside it. From the bank he wrenched a rock from the earth and let it go. It drifted slowly up into the air.

'The rock is really light around here, so if you pull it out of the ground, it just floats away. I guess the mountains must have broken free, just like that rock.' He shrugged, jumping back into the cart. 'Or maybe it's magic . . . '

'Well, it's certainly more dramatic than anything on the Rock of Sighs,' Thea laughed.

As the farmer's wagon continued in the

shadow of the mountains, the trees eventually made way for small cottages and fields of produce. Soon they were surrounded by life in a small, bustling village. Children played in the streets, which were full of market traders selling their wares. People actually seemed happy and safe – a far cry from the misery in Quinn's village. Perhaps harbouring a Dragon Knight wasn't as bad as people made out.

'Hillshade, next stop,' the farmer called. 'You'll find your blacksmith here.'

As Quinn jumped down and walked in the direction the farmer had pointed, Thea flicked him a silver coin and thanked him. He frowned slightly.

'Those black tunics of yours —' he began.

'None of your business!' Thea replied indignantly, hurrying away from the wagon and down the street.

'What was that about?' Quinn asked.

'I don't know,' said Thea. 'But we'd better find this Dragon Knight quickly. We don't want to be wandering around looking like trainees for much longer.'

They made their way down the street as the farmer headed back out of town.

'It's the same village we saw in the sword,' Quinn said. The village was in far better repair than Quinn's own. The houses all had iron bars on the windows and doors, and good, strong walls.

I'd like to see Goric try to kick those doors down, Quinn thought.

They followed the sword through the village as best they could. Quinn let it tug him in the right direction, holding it by his side so as few people would notice it as possible. The black-smith's shop was an unmistakable brick building in front of a public square near the middle of the village, with a tall chimney that was pouring out smoke.

'This must be it,' Thea muttered.

'Let's do this,' Quinn said.

He opened the door and an enormous wave of heat rolled over them. Sweat sprang out on Quinn's skin in seconds, soaking his tunic and trousers.

As they made their way inside, they spotted the blacksmith by the forge, hammering molten metal into submission. He looked even bigger in person than he had in the sword. His shoulders were as wide a bull's, and his arms were so thick with muscle they looked like tree trunks. Black, bristly stubble jutted from a rock-like jaw. He was hunched over his work, his face almost touching the belching flames, as he hammered away at a gigantic sword. The smith reached down and pumped the bellows and the flames roared up. Armour and weapons hung from the walls. The noise of the place was so deafening that he hadn't even noticed Quinn and Thea.

Quinn tilted his sword so that he could see the smith's reflection. 'It's him!' he whispered. Quinn saw the reflection of a gigantic red dragon, in the same way he'd seen his own dragonform reflected back at him.

As the light glanced off the blade the blacksmith noticed the disturbance and flicked his giant head round. Dropping the hammer and molten metal, he spun towards Quinn and Thea. His eyes widened and Quinn saw fire flash within them. He grabbed up a glowing poker and strode towards them.

'Who are you?' he growled, glaring at Quinn and Thea. 'What do you want?'

'W-we saw you in a sword,' Quinn stuttered. This wasn't the welcome he was expecting.

'You're guards!' the blacksmith roared, seeing what they were wearing. 'How did you —?'

'No!' Quinn shouted. 'We were looking for you . . . for the Dragon Knights . . . ' The huge blacksmith looming over him was just as terrifying as any member of the Black Guard and he didn't even have the magical armour.

At the mention of the Dragon Knights the blacksmith turned red with anger. The fury in his eyes shone as bright as the forge.

'You've got five seconds to explain yourselves,' he roared, 'or I'm going to throw you right out of that door.' The giant blacksmith reached for Quinn with one enormous, hairy hand.

'Dragonblood!' Quinn burst out.

'What did you say, boy?' the blacksmith boomed.

Quinn knew he shouldn't have said that, but it was too late. It was just like in the garrison: he was always saying things before he thought about them first. 'I have dragonblood. That's why we're here. We escaped from the Yaross Garrison to find you.'

The blacksmith froze, his fingers just an inch from Quinn's neck. He stared down at Quinn with fiery eyes. Then he sniffed at him suspiciously.

His face softened and he let his hands drop. 'Then I guess we'd better have a chat,' he said. 'Follow me.'

Quinn shot Thea a wary glance.

'Sparky fellow, isn't he?' Thea grinned.

'That's one way to describe him,' Quinn replied, sternly.

Ignus led them to a small, ramshackle cottage set behind the forge at a distance from its fiery flames. As Quinn settled himself awkwardly on the edge of the bed that filled up almost half the cottage, the blacksmith bustled around, pulling out cups and putting a kettle on the fire. Ignus was so tall he had to bend his head to stand up, and his shoulders looked like they were going to smash through the walls every time he turned. Ignus demanded Quinn tell him everything, and soon Quinn found himself detailing the escape from Yaross Garrison and his run-ins with Goric.

As he finished his tale, the door opened again, and a teenage boy and girl strode in. They looked so similar, with their long brown hair and stocky physique, Quinn thought they must be twins. They caught sight of Quinn and Thea and gave Ignus a curious look.

'It's all right,' Ignus mumbled. 'Show them what you can do, Areck.'

The boy shrugged then walked over to the cooking fire. He waved his hands over the heat, and the flames flared up. Quinn gasped. The boy just laughed, and twisted his hands, making the flames jump and dance before them all.

'Pretty good, huh?' he laughed.

He has dragonblood, too? Quinn thought. He looked over at Thea in amazement.

'Areck and Alysa,' Ignus said, introducing the twins. 'They're only just coming into their dragon powers.'

'How?' Quinn croaked. He'd thought all the dragonbloods were bound. He'd never expected to find them walking around freely. He'd thought he was the only one.

'Alysa is a tracker dragon,' Ignus said. 'She has superb tracking skills.'

'I can find anything and anyone,' she declared proudly. 'I even helped us find Ignus. That way we've managed to stay unbound.'

Quinn looked at Thea in amazement: a whole new generation of dragonbloods! They hadn't died out. He wondered how many more there might be out there. He felt a fierce delight burning up inside him. The Black Guard weren't being as successful as they thought.

'And now you, too. Sorry about the unfriendly reception,' Ignus said, looking rueful. 'I thought you must be spies from the Black Guard. No one's supposed to know I'm a flame dragon.' He glanced balefully at Alysa and Areck. 'Not that I'm much of one these days.'

'What happened to you?' Quinn asked.

'Well,' Ignus began, 'after the battle for the Imperial Castle the Dragon Knights went their separate ways: there was no use for us any more, Vayn's magic was too strong. I came to Yaross, as far away as I could get from his brutal power. The others spread out across the Islands, to live with the loss of their powers the best they could.'

'Was there nothing you could do?' Thea asked.

'I had no power . . . ' He pulled up his trouser leg to show a dull copper band clamped tight around his ankle. Thousands of tiny marks had been carved into the metal.

'Spells!' Thea leaned closer. 'I've never seen anything like them.'

'Vayn's dark magic,' Ignus explained. 'All the time we were protecting Emperor Marek, his own brother was learning the dark arts.' He shook his head. 'I **knew** he was resentful, but I never guessed he hated his own family so much.' He flicked the copper band with one enormous finger. A sickly purple light swirled over the surface then faded. 'These bands take away our ability to transform. I've tried everything I can to get it off, but it's impossible. No weapon can scratch it and no fire can scorch it. I've consulted every back-alley magician in the Twelve Islands, but none can break the enchantment.'

'Let me take a look,' Thea said.

Ignus shrugged. 'If you want.' He extended his leg.

Thea began to chant. Quinn felt magic gather and the air seemed to bend and shift. Purple, yellow and green sparks flickered around the copper band. Thea looked closely, then she shook her head and the magic faded.

'I'm sorry,' she said. 'It's far more advanced than anything I can deal with.'

Quinn stared at the band. Thea's magic was so much more powerful than Aunt Marta's, and this was beyond even her. He shuddered, thinking about Vayn. The man had defeated even the

Dragon Knights with his dark magic. Quinn could hardly imagine how much power the Emperor must have.

'You two,' Ignus said, jerking his head towards Areck and Alysa. 'Go and check the perimeter. From what Thea has said, the Black Guard will be looking for them.'

When the twins had gone, Ignus leaned close in to Quinn. 'I understand you're a dragonblood. I can smell it on you, and my nose never lies. I understand you're fleeing the Black Guard. But I just have one question for you, boy.' His fiery eyes bored into Quinn's. 'What exactly are you doing with the Emperor Marek's sword?'

Quinn looked down to where the golden sword lay beside him on the bed.

'My aunt gave it to me. She said it was my father's.'

Thea peered at the sword, frowning. 'You know, there's some half-complete magic on this sword. Maybe if we can finish the spell, it'll give us some answers.' She looked up at Quinn. 'Is that all right?'

'I guess,' Quinn said. Marta had been hiding stuff from him all his life, and the Black Guard had taken him before she could start to tell him the truth. There was just too much he didn't know.

'Good.' Thea sat up. 'Let me try something Telemus once showed me – but it might not be pretty.'

'OK,' Quinn said, 'whatever it takes.'

'In that case, give me the sword.'

'What are you going to do with it?' Quinn said, passing it to her.

'This.' She dropped the sword in the fire. The metal hissed and sang.

'What the —?' Quinn started.

'Shh,' Thea interrupted. 'We're looking into the sword's past . . . '

Quinn looked on as Thea began chanting a spell under her breath. The smoke from the fire began to churn and the flames spat multi-coloured sparks that swirled in ever-changing patterns. Slowly, a scene formed in the smoke. Ignus leaned over Quinn's shoulder, squinting at the emerging picture.

Quinn had seen this before. It was the Imperial Castle just after the dragons had fallen. Vayn's magical fog billowed up to engulf the Dragon Knights and send them crashing down to the earth. Quinn heard Ignus suck in a pained breath. But the scene didn't stay focused on the dragons. This time it swept past and around the castle to a small door in the wall which now stood open and through which people were fleeing. A woman came running out, a baby in her arms tightly wrapped in blankets. In one of her hands she was carrying the golden sword.

As she fled the castle, the woman muttered a spell. The golden sword shrank until it was no more than an emerald-handled knife. She dropped it into a pouch, and then shoved the pouch deep into the baby's blankets.

'One day, you can use this to return to your rightful place, Your Majesty,' the woman whispered to the sleeping baby.

Then she looked up and Quinn rocked back in shock. She was younger and she didn't look so frail, but the woman was Marta, without a doubt.

'Th-that's my aunt,' Quinn stuttered. 'That's Marta.' He turned to stare at the others in amazement. 'She was the one who brought me to Yaross. She gave me the sword.'

Quinn's mind whirred. *If Marta had been the one fleeing the castle, that must make me . . . the baby?*

Ignus dropped to his knees. 'Your Imperial Highness,' he boomed, bowing his head. 'You have returned.'

CHAPTER 14

A NEW ERA

Quinn couldn't help himself. His eyes bulged
and his jaw hung open.

That probably wasn't what the rightful
Emperor of Alariss was supposed to do, but
then only a few days ago he'd been an orphan
being raised by a washerwoman. Now Ignus
was telling him he was the true Emperor.

'What are you talking about?' Quinn gasped.

Ignus couldn't contain his excitement. He
stomped around the small cottage, almost
shaking the roof with his footsteps.

'You are the true son of Emperor Marek, the

148

great Earth Dragon!' he cried. 'You are the one I swore to serve and protect! I failed you then, but I will not fail you again!' He slapped a hand against the wall, causing a cup to fall from a shelf. 'Ha! Now Vayn will see! Now he will regret it!' He grabbed Quinn and shook him so hard his teeth rattled. 'You are the heir to the throne. You are the Emperor!'

The heir to the throne? How can I be?

'Don't be ridiculous!' Quinn cried, his mind whirring. Just because he had the Emperor's sword, surely that couldn't make him the son of the Emperor. 'But my father was a fisherman. He and my mother drowned at sea,' Quinn said desperately. His skin began to feel hot, just like it had done when the Black Guard had burned down Marta's house. A wisp of smoke rose from his tunic.

Ignus looked at him gravely. 'Emperor Marek and Empress Isaria drowned at sea too, and it was no accident. Vayn was behind it.'

Thea was staring at him with a glint in her eyes. 'I think it's all beginning to make sense, *Your Majesty*.'

Quinn blushed. 'Don't do that,' he said. He couldn't cope with Thea of all people treating him like an emperor. He wasn't the Emperor, even if his father had been. He was just a boy hiding from the Black Guard.

'That's why the sword came to life in your hand,' Thea said thoughtfully, looking at the golden blade. 'This is the sword the real Emperor used – it must only work with the rightful heir.'

'In fact,' Thea continued, 'that sword would have been used to knight the Dragon Knights. It bound them to him.'

'And to his heirs,' Ignus said.

'I wonder . . . ' Thea said, with the sparkle of an idea in her eye. 'Maybe we could use it to bind the Dragon Knights to you again. That might undo Vayn's spell and release them.'

'I'm supposed to free the Dragon Knights?' Quinn cried, unable to believe what he was hearing.

At that moment, the door burst open. Ignus swung around, his gigantic hands clenching to fists. He dropped them as Areck and Alysa ran in.

'There are Black Guard approaching the village!' Alysa said. 'Lots of them. They're looking for you two.'

Quinn stared at Thea. 'How did they know we were here?'

'The farmer who gave us a lift,' she said. 'He must have given us away!'

'Whoever told them, we have to hide you. Right away,' said Areck.

'Too late,' Ignus growled. 'The Guard know that Quinn and Thea are here.' He dropped to his knees in front of Quinn and bowed his head. 'There's only one thing that will save us. You must knight me!'

Quinn stumbled back. 'What?'

'Knight me! Swear me to service and free me.'

Quinn glanced at Thea. 'But how are you supposed to knight someone?'

'I don't know; you're the heir!' Thea said. 'Maybe put your sword across his shoulders and say he's your knight? And try not to slice him in two . . . '

'There's got to be more to it than that,'

Quinn said. 'Shouldn't there be a whole lot of vows and promises, and a whopping great ceremony?'

'Please, Your Majesty!' Ignus said. 'Hurry.'

Quinn cleared his throat – he couldn't help feeling how ridiculous this was. He was just a kid from an insignificant village on the poorest of the Twelve Islands. There had to be some mistake. He couldn't go around knighting people.

However, if the Black Guard were on their way, there might not be another choice. He took a deep breath and laid the flat of the blade across Ignus's shoulder. For a second, nothing happened; Quinn felt like an idiot, standing there pretending to be an emperor.

But then, the sword began to glow, just gently at first, but then with a more powerful light. Golden rays spilled from the blade, illuminating the small cottage like an otherworldly forge. Quinn raised a hand to shield his eyes, but then grew used to the strange light. Something seemed to stir inside him, just like when the dragon scales had appeared on his chest. From nowhere, words rushed from his lips in a language he'd never heard before. Somehow, he knew it was the ancient language of the dragons.

'By the power of dragonblood and in the sight of the gods,' the words rang out, 'I bind you to protect the Twelve Islands against all threat and I bind your loyalty to the true Emperor. Advance, Ignus, Dragon Knight of the Twelve Islands.'

With a crack, the manacle fell from Ignus's ankle and clanged to the ground. Ignus snatched it up and tossed it angrily into the fire. It sizzled and blazed with a magical purple flame. Streamers of heat lashed up the chimney like whips. Quinn backed away.

'At last!' Ignus bellowed. 'After all this time. Free!'

He rolled his mighty shoulders and roared. The air shimmered around him, blurring his hair and skin and clothes.

'Uh-oh,' Quinn muttered.

Ignus seemed to stretch and grow. Inside the flickering air, his limbs twisted. Flashes of red lightning cascaded over his body. His head pressed against the roof and his shoulders pushed against the walls. Beams creaked. Dust rained down.

'You might want to get out of here,' Areck cried.

Quinn grasped Thea. 'Let's go!'

He shoved her towards the door and raced after her.

A thick tail erupted from Ignus's back as he leaned forward. It smacked into Quinn, knocking his legs away and throwing him to the floor. His head bounced off the flagstones. He gritted his teeth and stumbled to his feet. Thea grabbed him and hauled him through the doorway, right after Areck and Alysa.

Just in time.

Wings burst from Ignus's scaled body. His back arched up. Plaster crumbled from the walls. The iron bars that secured the door and windows popped suddenly, spinning across the village street. Timbers snapped.

Quinn threw himself down, dragging Thea

with him, as the small house exploded behind them. Debris rained down and over them.

Quinn rolled onto his back and stared at what was left of the house. A gigantic red dragon reared up, shrugging off the last remnants of wood, mud and straw. Its wings spread out over the neighbouring houses. The dragon's neck stretched up above the village, reaching at least three storeys high. Burning eyes stared down. Great claws pawed at the hard earth. The wings flapped once, and the wind almost sent Quinn and Thea tumbling across the ground.

Ignus the Flame Dragon tipped back his head and roared. A stream of fire burned hundreds of yards up into the air. The enormous dragon launched itself upwards, trailing smoke and dirt behind him.

'The Flame Dragon,' Quinn gasped. 'He's returned!'

CHAPTER 15

THE RETURN OF THE DRAGONS

Quinn stared in wonder as Ignus soared into the air. The only time he'd seen a dragon was in the mists of Marta's spell. He'd had no way of knowing just how enormous and terrifying a real Dragon Knight would be. The dragon twisted and turned in the air; he flapped his leathery wings like a bird released from its cage, soaring higher and higher until he disappeared into a bank of cloud.

One day I'll be like that . . . Quinn thought.

'So much for hiding,' Thea said. 'They'll have seen that ten miles away . . . '

Footsteps and shouts sounded. A crowd of

villagers emerged from the houses and the streets and came running towards Ignus's ruined cottage, congregating in Hillshade's main square.

'What did I tell you?' Thea laughed.

Suddenly Quinn was snapped back to reality. *What was Ignus thinking?*

'The Guard's horses are stationed at a tavern just a mile up the road,' Areck cried.

'They're coming for us!' Quinn shouted.

There was no way Goric and the Black Guard could have missed that show. Thea and Quinn would be hauled back to the garrison – or worse.

'What happened?' one of the villagers demanded. 'Where's Ignus?'

'We saw the cottage explode!' another said.

Quinn looked desperately around. If news got back to Emperor Vayn he'd send more than just Yaross Garrison after him. Ignus couldn't defeat Vayn on his own, and Quinn had no idea how to use his own dragon powers. He didn't even know what his powers *were*.

'Um . . . the sun . . . ' Quinn tried. 'There were these red flares and . . . '

But he didn't get to finish. Enormous wings beat the air above him, like the giant rattle of thunder in a storm. Ignus dived from the air and landed in the village square, right next to Quinn. The ground underneath shook like an earthquake.

'Or, you know, a dragon,' Quinn muttered. *Great*.

He looked up at Ignus; he didn't even come up to the dragon's knee. Ignus could have leaned over and squashed him flat. He wouldn't need the fire or those claws that could cut a bear in half.

Then the dragon lowered his scaly head and bowed to the villagers, smoke drifting down over them. Ignus's head was as big as a cart, and his teeth could have crunched through an oak tree, but, surprisingly, none of the villagers seemed scared. None of them were backing away or running off to report Ignus to the Black Guard. One of the men even laughed. He stepped forward and clapped Ignus soundly on the neck.

'At last!' the villager shouted.

'I apologise,' Ignus said, seriously. His deep voice sounded like he was chewing on gravel. 'I got carried away. It has been too long since I was a dragon.' He stretched out his wings and the crowd cheered.

'We never believed the Dragon Knights killed the Emperor Marek,' another villager said. 'We know Ignus. He'd never do something like that.'

Thea stepped forward. 'It's true. The Dragon Knights didn't betray the Imperial Family. Vayn did. He killed the Emperor and Empress and took the Twelve Islands of Alariss for himself. He said the Dragon Knights had murdered the whole Imperial Family so that people would turn against them, but he lied. And he lied about the true heir being killed.' She turned to Quinn. '*This* is your Emperor. This is Marek's true heir!'

The villagers stared at Quinn in complete disbelief. Quinn didn't blame them. He knew he didn't *look* like an emperor. He looked like a peasant in a shabby, torn version of the Black Guard's tunic and trousers. He wouldn't have believed it either. He still wasn't sure he did. He felt his body burn with heat again, but this time it was because he was blushing all the way from his feet up to the roots of his hair.

'This *boy*?' a villager shouted, mockingly.

'Show them the sword,' Thea whispered.

Quinn gulped, but he pulled out his father's sword and held it up in the air. Golden light blazed from it again.

Gasps sounded from the crowd – some people even bowed before him. Quinn felt himself blush even more. It felt weird that people were bowing to him. *He* was the one who spent his life bowing to other people. He'd spent so much time with his head pressed into the dirt he almost had a permanently black mark on his forehead. Suddenly the thought of being back with Marta in their little cottage didn't seem so bad. All he had to complain about there was damp laundry.

Except Marta had given up everything for him, and the Black Guard were trying to kill him. They treated everyone like scum. *It's not right*, he thought. *Someone needs to do something.* He gathered up his courage.

'Stand up,' he called to the villagers. Slowly, nervously, they got to their feet. 'You've bowed to other people for too long,' he said. 'The Black Guard might want you to put your faces in the dirt, but I don't.' He lifted the sword again. 'Ignus, Thea and I will take the Empire back from Vayn again,' he shouted. 'We will lift this evil from you!'

Ignus shook his enormous red head. 'We will, but not yet. Not while this village remains defenceless. When the Black Guard come and they discover the village has sheltered a Dragon Knight and the true Emperor, they will kill everyone in it. I cannot allow that to happen. We must move carefully. The Black Guard cannot know.'

He'd hardly finished speaking when a cry started further up in the village.

'The Black Guard! They're coming!'

CHAPTER 16

FLIGHT AND FIGHT

Ignus transformed in an instant. His dragonform fell away in a rush of air. Scales faded into skin and his wings and tail withdrew. Within moments, the blacksmith was standing there, staring at the burning wreckage of his cottage from the village square.

'Fetch buckets,' Areck shouted. 'We may be able to hide Ignus's transformation yet.'

'If they find a dragon in our village they'll tear us to pieces,' Alysa cried.

As the band of guards approached the village, the villagers tossed buckets of water and sand onto the cottage. At the sight of the twenty-strong Black Guard they dropped their buckets and bowed. Quinn, Thea and Ignus dropped beside them.

Some of the guards dismounted and looked suspiciously on the burning wreckage of the building, but they didn't give the villagers permission to rise. Beside him, Quinn felt the heat coming off Ignus in waves as the villagers cowered in fear.

Two of the Guard kicked their way through the ruins, lifting up charred timbers and shoving aside collapsed walls. Quinn recognised them as Jarin and Rowena and cursed under his breath.

'What's happened here?' Jarin demanded. 'What is capable of such destruction?'

'An accident.' Ignus rose from the ground to address them. It looked like he was trying to steer them away from Quinn and Thea.

'A likely story,' Rowena grunted. 'We're looking for two runaway trainees from the Guard. Maybe they had something to do with it?' She turned to look at the villagers. 'We were told they were here. You will turn them over to us now or you will all pay the price. Prove your loyalty, or die!'

None of the villagers moved. They kept their faces pressed into the dirt.

Quinn looked down, desperate not to be spotted. *The villagers are risking their lives for us,* he thought. *If we don't do something they'll be killed!*

When no one spoke, Rowena gestured to Jarin and the rest of the small band. 'Separate the children. We'll check them one at a time. And then . . . ' she laughed, 'we'll kill them one at a time. We'll soon see how long their silence lasts.'

Jarin moved through the crowd, hauling young children away from their parents and shoving them to stand on the other side of the street. Quinn and Thea exchanged a helpless look – it was only a matter of time before he'd reach them.

Suddenly the sound of horses' hooves echoed down the street; a cloud of dust rose from the road. Quinn's heart sank as the dirt haze cleared and he saw the familiar figure of Captain Goric ride into the village. Quinn gestured to Thea and together they tried to merge with the crowd of villagers. Quinn prayed that someone would cause a diversion. Maybe they would be able to sneak away.

Goric leapt from his horse and stamped over to the children. His eyes were wild with fury.

'Where are they?' he demanded.

The children looked on, bewildered. Some of them started to sob.

On the far side of the road, Quinn saw Ignus getting angrier and angrier. His hands were clenching and unclenching; the big muscles in his shoulders were heaving under his shirt. Steam drifted from his mouth up into the hot air.

Goric grabbed a boy from the crowd and leaned in close, his face twisting in a menacing scowl. The boy couldn't have been more than seven years old. Goric hoisted him up into the air and drew his sword.

'Someone is going to tell me!' Goric shouted. 'Or you will watch this boy die.'

NO!

Quinn knew he had no choice. He couldn't let Goric kill the boy. He took a step forward and pushed his way through the crowds.

'We're here!' he shouted desperately.

Goric turned to where Quinn was standing and dropped the boy on the dirt. His eyes flashed like a weary predator who'd finally spotted its prey.

'You!' he sneered as he marched over, sword held high in the air. Never mind returning to the garrison, Quinn would be killed.

But before Goric had a chance to grab Quinn by the throat, there was a gigantic roar from the crowd of villagers.

'Ignus, wait!' Quinn shouted, but it was too late.

Ignus tipped back his head. A torrent of smoke exploded out of his mouth. An inhuman bellow erupted from his throat and there, in front of the Black Guard, Ignus transformed.

'What?' Goric cursed. 'It can't be!'

The guards stumbled back in shock. There

hadn't been a full-grown dragon in the Islands for twelve years. Most of the guards had never seen one, and they'd never expected to face a real Dragon Knight.

Ignus turned on them. Fire ripped from his throat, tearing into a group of guards. They fell back, screaming. Ignus roared again, leaping forward. Claws flashed out, ripping through the magical black armour with a devastating screech of tearing metal. The armour could stop most weapons, but it was no match for a furious dragon.

The guards fell back, shouting and yelling, but none of them were willing to approach Ignus, and Quinn didn't blame them. They spent their time bullying villagers, stealing and executing unarmed peasants. Now, suddenly, they were faced with a real foe.

With a beat of his wings, Ignus lifted off the ground, sending dust swirling across the square. He swooped above the village, blowing carefully directed bursts of fire over the guards. Quinn watched as he saw Rowena burst into flames, her armour no match for Ignus's power.

'Woah!' Thea gasped.

Goric screamed with rage and went on the offensive. He had been in Vayn's army when they had taken the Imperial Castle and he'd fought Dragon Knights before – there was no way he'd let Ignus get away without a fight.

'Attack formation!' he shouted, raising his magical shield. 'To me!'

Guards came running and formed a wedge behind Goric. His magical sword glittered frosty and blue in the air.

Ignus swooped down. His claws grasped a group of guards attempting to shelter behind the houses and tossed them over the roofs. Quinn saw the familiar figure of Jarin go flying through the air and come crashing down like a sack of potatoes.

'Forward!' Goric screamed. His formation of Black Guard advanced, hiding behind their shields. Archers raced to their flanks, notching arrows to their strings.

Ignus swung around and sent a blast of fire towards them. Goric lifted his shield. Magic sparkled, and the fire cascaded off it, burning the ground around the guards, but leaving Goric unharmed. His cruel face twisted into a laugh.

'The Emperor has not left us defenceless against your evil, Dragon Knight,' Goric shouted. Behind him, his men loosed their arrows. One bounced from Ignus's thick scales, but the other lodged in one of his wings. He let out another roar of fury.

Quinn turned to see Areck and Alysa transform. Areck's body twisted and jerked. Heat rose from him in waves. In seconds, a flame dragon crouched on the street, like Ignus, but smaller. Alysa bent over, and her body elongated and darkened. She seemed to flicker, as though mist was drifting between her and Quinn. She transformed into a stone-grey dragon and stood next to Areck, ready to fight.

The two dragons launched into the air to join Ignus.

Quinn and Thea watched in awe as the dragons joined forces against the Black Guard. Areck and Alysa weren't nearly as large or powerful as Ignus, but the Guard couldn't defend in three directions at once. Areck picked up a burning tree and dropped it into the formation of Black Guard, forcing them to scatter. Alysa dived down, snatching up the fleeing guards and dropping them from high above the village. Alysa, the tracker, had no problem twisting and turning the torrent of arrows, homing in on her next battle. Ignus's great bursts of flame sent whole groups of guards scurrying for cover.

But the guards with bows and arrows were causing trouble. The arrows had been magically enchanted, and they were firing harder and faster than ordinary arrows. The dragons had to dodge and twist in the air. Even if they missed on the way up, the arrows would pose a threat once more as they swooped back down.

Areck darted down onto the battlefield and opened his mouth, puffing out an enormous cloud of smoke. Alysa beat her wings and sent the swirling smoke across the battlefield. The blinding screen of fog hid the dragons from the guards, giving them a chance to mount a fresh attack.

'Take hostages!' Goric yelled to his men. 'Use villagers as shields.'

Quinn stared at Thea in horror.

'We've got to do something,' she shouted.

'Quick, to the forge . . . we have to arm them,' Quinn said.

Quinn and Thea ordered the villagers to try to reach Ignus's forge, running for their lives across the square and away from the guards.

Suddenly, Thea's magic surged ahead of them and something came flying through the air towards the crowd. Quinn blinked as a chain-mail shirt dropped over the head of the nearest villager. A moment later, a flurry of helmets spun across the street, landing on unsuspecting villagers' heads.

Thea was using her magic to arm the villagers. They had a chance to defend themselves.

The people of this village had risked their lives to protect him and Thea. If Quinn wanted to be Emperor he'd have to show the villagers he was worth it. He'd have to show them he was willing to risk his life for them as well.

As the Black Guard strode from the smoke towards the forge, Quinn drew his father's sword. His heart was pounding and heat was rushing over his skin. He gave a sideways glance to Thea, who'd salvaged a small sword and dagger from Ignus's forge.

'Let's do this,' she cried.

'For the Twelve Islands!' Quinn yelled.

He launched himself at the Black Guard.

The first guardsman lumbered towards Quinn, shouting. The heavy sword came down, but Quinn was already dodging to the side. His golden sword whipped out, catching the guardsman under the arm, clanging against the armour and sending the guardsman to the ground. Two more stepped in front of him. Quinn slashed at them and they fell back. Sweat dripped in his eyes and his dark hair flapped across his forehead. He spun, hacking at the next guardsman. Smoke rushed across them, and Quinn charged forward.

The guards had their magical black armour and years of training, but Quinn had always been fast, and his father's sword seemed alive in his hand. It was like it knew what to do before Quinn did. It scarcely weighed anything as it swished through the air.

A guard reached for one of the villagers. She tried to defend herself with the spear she'd picked up, but the guardsman sliced it in two with his sword. Quinn leapt on the man's armoured back and brought the hilt of his sword crashing down on his helmet. The dragon-shaped hilt flashed as magic collided with magic. The guard went clanging to the ground in a heap.

Quinn charged once more. *So this is what it's like to be a Dragon Knight,* he thought, *fighting against anyone who threatened the people of the Twelve Islands!* Power seemed to race up and down his arms. He turned, looking for more guards to fight – seeing Thea twist and turn in action, using her magic to protect the villagers.

'Quinn!' a harsh voice snarled.

Quinn snapped around to see Goric stalking

towards him. His face was twisted into a mad smile. His helmet was missing and blood was dripping from a cut above his eye, but his sword was covered in blood too.

'There you are, you wretched dog!' Goric shouted. 'How dare you leave the garrison? You should know there's no escaping us.'

This was it – Goric would try to end him once and for all.

'And you should know I'll never be a filthy guard,' Quinn cried. 'Not while I have dragon-blood coursing through my veins.'

Goric looked shocked and disgusted, his mouth twisting into a grimace. 'Dragonblood?' he sneered. 'Of course. I always said there was something wrong with you and now I know I was right.' He spat on the ground and paced towards Quinn, huge and menacing. 'The dragons were a curse on this land, boy. Forget being bound, I'm going to take your head and deliver it to your wretched aunt. Then she'll know what it means to conceal a dragon. Then she'll know the price for defying me!'

'In that case you'll be killing the true Emperor,' Quinn spat back.

'What?' Goric snapped.

Quinn flashed his sword at Goric. 'Recognise this?'

Goric looked like he'd seen the ghost of Emperor Marek himself. He seemed to sway slightly on his feet, as if his legs were about to give way. 'No,' he whispered. 'That sword was lost long ago . . . '

'And now it's back,' Quinn continued, 'along with the Dragon Knights. And soon, Emperor Vayn will be finished!'

'NEVER!' Goric exploded. He threw himself at Quinn, his sword flashing down. Quinn flicked his wrist and brought his blade up to block it, battering it away with all his force.

In a fury, Goric hacked at Quinn from every direction. Goric was faster and stronger than his men, and his sword glowed blue with frost. A single cut of it would turn Quinn to ice.

Quinn parried and twisted, using instinct to fend Goric off. It was one thing fighting him back at the garrison, but it was another to do it for real. This time he wouldn't just break his sword – he'd break his neck.

Goric cried out and swiped again, putting all his weight behind his weapon. Quinn brought his sword up, but Goric had caught him off balance and his ankle twisted under him. The force of the blow sent ripples of pain up through his sword and his arms, and suddenly, muscles convulsing with agony, his father's sword was knocked from his hand. It spun away into the smoke on the makeshift battlefield.

Goric let out a shriek of triumph.

'So much for dragonblood,' he cried, bringing his sword above Quinn's head.

Quinn stumbled in the dirt and threw up his hands as the sword came crashing down . . .

CHAPTER 17

THE END AND THE BEGINNING

Quinn braced himself for the impact and the searing pain. But as the sword came down he heard a clanging noise instead. He opened his eyes and watched as the sword bounced back up into the air. He looked down at his arm, where he'd expected shattered bone and blood. Instead, it was covered in smooth, golden dragon scales. Even Goric's magic sword couldn't pierce them.

Quinn felt a surge of power course through him.

Goric's mouth fell open in shock. Then he

snarled and lifted his sword again. 'Surrender or die!'

'I'll never surrender to you!' Quinn cried.

The golden scales had given him just the chance he needed. He scrambled to his feet and desperately swung at Goric with his open hand. His fingers scraped across Goric's face, gouging a bloody chunk out of the Captain. Goric reeled back, clutching his cheek.

Above, Quinn saw Ignus swooping and swirling, fire snorting from his nostrils like a volcano out of control.

'Ignus!' he called. 'Over here!'

The dragon wheeled in the sky, but not fast enough. Goric recovered and came at him once more, his face red with blood and rage.

Quinn darted across the ground as his scales faded and picked up his golden sword. As Goric tried to slash at him, Quinn turned and brought his blade down on Goric's armour. It cut through the magic metal with ease, leaving a bloodied gash across the chainmail.

'I am the true heir to the Twelve Islands,'

Quinn roared. 'And I say you're not welcome on Yaross any more.'

Goric was stunned. The terrifying scowl on his face was replaced by shock and fear. He was about to reply but before he could form the words a shadow appeared above him and plucked him from the ground like a vegetable from the dirt.

'Ignus!' Quinn cheered.

The flame dragon lifted Goric into the sky, his leathery wings carrying him upwards high above the village. With a twist of his powerful limbs, Ignus let him drop, flinging him towards the ground.

With a scream of anger and crunch of metal, Goric landed on the ground like a ragdoll.

Quinn stared in shock. He'd never thought he would see the end of Goric. For years the Captain had made his life hell and now he was defeated. A few days ago Quinn thought he was nothing special but now, as the final few scales faded from his arm, he felt proud. He had dragonblood – and it had saved his life.

'Quinn!'

snapped back to reality. *Thea!*

...!' she said, running over to him.

...ke from the battlefield cleared, the

...gan to cheer. Everywhere, the Black

Gua... ...re fleeing. Seeing their master defeated
and the resistance from the villagers, they'd lost
their nerve.

Quinn felt elation bubble up inside him until
he wanted to jump up and punch the air. 'We
did it!'

Thea beamed back at him.

Heavy wings beat above them as Ignus came
down to land on the street, transforming back
into his human form. The villagers crowded
round him with thanks.

'We have won this battle,' Ignus rumbled. 'We
should be proud, but I do not think this village
has seen the last of the Black Guard. This time
we caught them by surprise, but next time they
will be prepared.'

As if on cue, Quinn heard a whooshing noise
rising fast like a fire catching in a barn. He spun
around.

'I sense magic,' Thea cried. 'Something's happening!'

Purple flames leapt up from a pile of smouldering rubble. Quinn stumbled back, shielding his eyes. The flames rushed together and a fiery image appeared. Quinn saw a thin face marked with cruel scars and twisted lines. The dark, angry eyes flashed in the purple flame like a vicious animal's. The mouth was twisted into a sneer of hatred.

Emperor Vayn! Quinn recognised his gnarled face from flags and portraits around the island.

The Emperor's eyes fixed on Quinn and Ignus.

'Ignus!' the Emperor snarled. 'You should have stayed bound! You should have lived your pathetic, pointless life rather than dare to face me again!' His gaze shifted to Quinn, and his expression darkened. His lip curled like paper in a fire. 'Who are you, who dares to defy me . . . ?'

Quinn stared into the eyes of the man who had murdered his mother and father, and he felt fury build up in him again. 'I am the true heir!'

he shouted into the flames. 'You killed my parents.'

The flames hissed and spluttered with magical rage.

'You survived?' Vayn cried. 'I thought you had drowned with them.'

'You thought wrong, Vayn,' Quinn shouted.

'No matter,' Vayn continued, his anger sending purple flames across the rubble. 'I will make you wish you *had* drowned. You think freeing a Dragon Knight will save you?'

'No,' Quinn admitted. 'But once I free all six, we will save the Twelve Islands together.'

'I defeated all six in one battle!' Vayn laughed darkly. 'You will never reclaim the throne. I will send a thousand Black Guard against you! Cut your own throat now, boy – before I cut it for you!'

With a hiss, the purple flames exploded into the air and the magical image of Emperor Vayn spun away.

Quinn felt fear try to rise inside him, but seeing Vayn made him determined. He squeezed the fear down. He wouldn't let it beat him.

'All of Vayn's Guard will come looking for us,' Ignus rumbled. 'This is the first place they will come. The village isn't safe any more.'

Quinn raised his chin. 'We have to take the fight to Vayn. We can't just wait for him to attack. We should find the other Dragon Knights and release them. That way we'll have a chance.'

'I agree,' Thea added. 'There's no other choice.'

Ignus looked uneasily around the village.

'I cannot leave these people undefended. Ordinary men and women cannot stand against the Black Guard.'

'They won't have to,' Thea said, stepping out in front of Ignus. 'Areck and Alysa have come into their dragon powers. They can defend the village! The Black Guard want you and Quinn. They might want to punish the villagers, but they're not going to go up against two dragons to do it, not when we're getting away.'

Ignus still looked unsure. 'You underestimate

the Black Guard. This village is too hard to defend.'

'Then we'll move to the Floating Mountains,' Areck said.

Alysa chipped in. 'There must be enough space up there. There's water and land; the villagers can farm and build houses and they'll have us for protection.'

Ignus thought for a moment, then nodded. 'As you wish. Areck and Alysa will stay to protect the villagers and take them to the foothills of the mountains. I will go with Quinn to my brothers of old.'

'And me!' Thea chimed in. 'We've come this far already . . .'

Quinn smiled. It felt good to have a magician and a dragon on his side.

'Very well,' Ignus said.

'The villagers will be safe in the mountains,' Areck continued.

Ignus nodded his gigantic head. 'But nowhere is truly safe while Vayn still rules the Islands.'

'Then we'll find the rest of the Dragon

Knights,' Quinn said. 'One Dragon Knight might be no match for the Guard, but six of them? We might just do it!'

He picked his father's sword out of the dust and held it up. The reflection in the blade formed an image. It showed a misty marshland. Ominous shadows stretched across the landscape like long fingers.

'That's Keriss Island,' Thea said. 'There must be a Dragon Knight there.'

'Then that's where we'll go,' Quinn said.

As the villagers called their goodbyes, Ignus transformed once more. Quinn and Thea scrambled up onto his broad, scaled back and tucked themselves in the space between his shoulders. The dragon's great wings beat, and they were up off the ground and flying high in the evening sky.

Below, the smoking ruins of the village slipped away. Quinn felt the rush of air through his hair. One day soon, he would fly like this, and he would bring freedom back to the Twelve Islands.

Emperor Vayn had ruled with cruelty and greed for twelve long years. That was twelve years too many. Now, at last, the Dragon Knights were fighting back.

This battle might be over, but Quinn's adventure had only just begun . . .

\

DRAG⊕N
KNIGHTS

IGNUS THE FLAME DRAGON

DRAGONFORM

An enormous dragon with bright red scales the colour of burnt rubies, a crested head and flame-coloured eyes.

BACKGROUND

Twelve years ago, in the days of Emperor Marek, Ignus lived on the Imperial Isle at the castle garrison, guarding the Imperial family. When Vayn killed his own brother and denied the Dragon Knights their power, he and the other knights fled to the four corners of the empire to escape imprisonment or death at the hands of the Black Guard.

OCCUPATION

Blacksmith in Hillshade, a small village on Yaross.

DRAGON
KNIGHTS

ATTRIBUTES

Big, burly Ignus is as strong as an ox, even in his human
form. He is fiercely loyal but often quick to let his fiery
temper get the better of him. However, this belies a softer
nature, and he is always on hand to give guidance and help.

STRENGTHS

As a Flame Dragon, Ignus is part of a long line of dragons
stretching as far back as there has been magic in the Islands
of Alariss. He is master of the devastating power of fire,
which he can use to sear through the strongest Black Guard
armour.

WEAKNESSES

As one of the heaviest Dragon Knights, with a muscly
dragonform, he's slower in the air than the some of the
lighter, more nimble fliers. This leaves him prone to the
Black Guards' magically strengthened arrows as they come
hurtling through the skies.

DRAG⊕N
KNIGHTS

READ ON FOR MORE
DRAGON KNIGHTS ADVENTURES

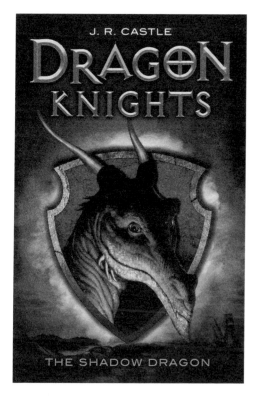

CHAPTER I

RAGING WATERS

Quinn stood on the ship's foredeck while the storm raged all around him. Lightning crashed through the sky, splitting the clouds and flickering white light across the dark waves. Rain lashed into his face. Every time the ship was driven into the mountainous waves the impact made his teeth judder, and great sheets of spray surged across the deck. His clothes were soaked through and his hands were freezing where he gripped the wooden rail.

He'd been on the merchant ship, the *Seagull*, for two days now, ploughing his way through the storms that plagued the seas between Yaross and Keriss Islands. The days and nights merged into one now that summer had turned into a brutal, storm-laden autumn, and everything was shrouded in fog. But despite the rough conditions, Quinn preferred it up on deck.

'Damn it!' he cursed, dodging another wave that came crashing over his feet, soaking his legs. A voice called from above him as he grabbed onto the rigging.

'You, boy!' the voice growled. 'Get below deck!'

Quinn could just make out the shadowy figure of the captain's mate, high in his crow's nest. Quinn mouthed a reply to suggest he couldn't hear above the shrieking of the rain, and pulled his wind-blown hood back over his head, ignoring him. Even though Thea, his fellow runaway, and Ignus, the Dragon Knight, would be down there, all he wanted right now was the fresh air and the wind.

Just a few weeks ago he'd been an orphan living with his aunt in a tiny village on Yaross, the least important of the Twelve Islands of Alariss. It wasn't until he'd been forced to join the Black Guard trainees and he discovered he had dragon-blood – with the power to morph from a human into a fearsome dragon – that he'd had to run away.

Quinn had grown up believing that the Dragon Knights had betrayed the Imperial Family and murdered them; but it was all a big lie. His aunt, Marta, had shown him the truth. The person who had really murdered the Emperor and Empress was Vayn, the Emperor's own brother. And even more difficult to believe, the Emperor and Empress were his parents and he, Quinn, was now the true Emperor.

Lightning flashed again, casting pink and purple forks of electricity pulsing across the sky. Quinn flinched and wrapped his cloak more tightly around him, gripping the wooden railing until his knuckles turned white. He heard the captain's mate hollering again from above.

Back in Yaross Quinn and Thea had managed to escape the Black Guard and use Quinn's magical sword to free the first of the Dragon Knights,

Ignus, the Flame Dragon. Together they had helped to free Ignus's village from the Black Guard's tyranny, but Emperor Vayn had discovered what they'd done all too quickly.

That was why Quinn, Ignus and Thea had to bribe their way onto the *Seagull*: they were keeping a low profile until they were strong enough to face Vayn. Now Quinn spent his days deep in thought, Ignus made friends with the rowdy sailors and Thea practised her magic spells in a quiet corner.

The storm winds thrummed madly through the ship's rigging, battering the creaking vessel into the gigantic waves. The clouds above were black as the gods' rage.

'Quinn?' a voice shouted through the howl of the storm.

Quinn turned, half-expecting to see the grizzled face of an angry sailor. Instead, blinking the rain out of her eyes, Thea was staggering up from below deck and clutching on to a line. She tried to shield herself from the whipping rain, her bright red hair clinging to her face as she struggled to find her feet.

'What are you doing up here?' she shouted.

Quinn reached out for her as she traversed the slippery deck. 'I'm thinking,' he called.

'Try thinking down below, you idiot!' Thea shrieked, stretching for his fingertips. 'There's less chance of being struck by lightning!'

Thea grabbed out towards Quinn and hauled herself up beside him, against the angle of the towering waves.

'And more chance of losing my temper with those sailors . . .' Quinn replied. Earlier, Quinn and Thea had been playing cards with the sailors below deck, but the cheating captain had got the fiery dragonblood coursing through Quinn's veins once more. It was only a game, but Quinn couldn't control it. It was a good job all he could muster was a golden talon or two. If he'd turned into a dragon the size of Ignus, the whole ship would have gone down.

'Dragonform getting to you?' Thea asked. 'It'll just take time – my magic didn't come overnight . . .'

'It's not just that,' Quinn shrugged awkwardly,

although he did wish he had more control over his dragon abilities. 'It's my parents.' He peered out over the rail at the heaving, dark water. Wind thrashed the top of the waves into foamy white crests and sent spray lashing through the air. 'This is where they drowned – just off the coast of Keriss. Aunt Marta told me they were fishing . . .'

But she'd been lying, protecting him from the Black Guard. And yet it still hurt that she hadn't told him the truth. *She could have trusted me*, he thought.

'. . . But they weren't fishing,' Thea said. 'They were the Emperor and Empress.'

Quinn nodded. 'Whatever they were doing out here, they didn't just sink – Vayn must have sabotaged their ship. My father was a dragon-blood. He could have got out of there when it started to sink, but he didn't . . .' He stared gloomily into the water as it surged and fell away beneath them, raising the ship up and then dropping it down with a thump that shook the timbers. 'Their ship is still down there somewhere.'

Once again he was snapped out of his thoughts by the captain's mate barking from above.

'Land ahoy!' the sailor roared from his crow's nest. 'Beware the rocks!'

Shouts and crashes sounded across the ship. Quinn's amber eyes flashed. *Rocks?* For a moment he imagined their own ship going down in these stormy seas, the cold waves crashing over the side, the planks splitting and breaking apart and the angry water closing over them . . .

Sailors came hurrying up from the hatches and raced for the lines; some of the ropes were as thick as Quinn's arm. Ignus stamped up behind them, his face a sickly green. When he wasn't playing cards with the sailors down below trying to distract himself, he'd been curled up on his bunk. Apparently flame dragons didn't mix too well with water.

'What's happening?' Quinn shouted as Ignus stumbled up to them uneasily. For such a big, strong man, he was clearly lacking sea legs.

'We're almost at Keriss harbour,' Ignus rumbled in reply, running a hand across his stubbly chin.

'Thank the Heavens. Look.' He pointed a thick finger ahead of them.

The clouds and mist slowly began to lift, giving the voyagers a better view of where they were heading. However, what Quinn saw didn't fill him with confidence. Rocks jutted out from the waves like a dragon's talons, curving high above the ship's mast; a narrow channel snaked its way between the cliffs to clear water beyond with the port in the distance. Water whirled through the channel – it looked like a shipwreck waiting to happen.

'We make for the Kerissian Pass! All hands on deck!' the captain called, grabbing the helm from a lowly member of the crew. The rest of the sailors manned their stations, pulling at ropes and bustling around on deck.

'Are they crazy?' Thea shouted up at Ignus. 'We'll never make it through there.'

'It's the only way,' Ignus bellowed back. 'You might want to hang on. This is going to get choppy!'

The sailors eased out the sails as far as they would go as the wind came around behind them; the ship ran before the wind, heading right for the cliffs, picking up speed. The captain seemed to be having trouble controlling its direction as they raced over the waves. Shouts and yells sounded as the sailors struggled to manage their lines. The curving talons of rock seemed to close in over the ship as it headed for the entrance to the harbour. Quinn was sure he could reach out and brush his fingers against them as the sharp rocks sliced by.

'It's not wide enough,' he groaned.

'Hang on!' Thea cried.

As if in response, a gust of wind sent their ship slipping sideways towards one of the towering rocks. Quinn yelled in surprise, but the next moment the sailors were hauling on a line, pulling a sail across, and the ship darted in the other direction.

A sudden swirl in the wind sent the sail on the port side snapping across the deck – the wooden boom splintered like a matchstick. With a yell, a sailor holding his line was sent spinning over the planks to crash into the guardrail. The line he'd been holding slashed back and forth in the air as the sail snapped loosely from the mast. Immediately, the ship lost speed and began to drift, driven by the running waves.

Quinn and Thea stared in horror as the ship lurched directly towards a jagged spike of rock that rose up from the waves like a spear.

'No!' Quinn yelled. 'It's going to crash . . .!'